Princess Rose and the Quest of the Golden Gown

By

Jennifer and Daniel Frazier

Ralph,
Thank you for all
the laughs in this most
effed-up year of our
Lord Shezmu.
We hope Olivia
enjoys the book.
LMB

"Jennifer from
Kentucky"

ISBN: 978-1-7352958-0-0 (Paperback)
ISBN: 978-1-7352958-1-7 (Digital)

Any references to historical events, real people, or real places are used fictitiously. Names, characters, and places are products of the author's imagination.

Cover image by Catalina Murcia Alejo.
Interior art by Daniel Frazier.
Book design by Daniel Frazier.

Printed in the United States of America.

First printing edition 2020.

Jennifer and Daniel Frazier
112 Hamlin Way
Lawrenceburg, KY 40342

www.ametheria.com

For Morgan and Stephen

Table of Contents

Prologue

The young woman sewed alone by the fire. The night was cold, and the small hut where she worked swayed slightly as the wind blew, but her father had built the simple structure to be sturdy, and the drafts that eased in were no match for the warmth around the hearth. She wiped her eyes as she thought of her father. Sickness had taken both her parents the previous winter just before she turned sixteen, and being an only child left her lonely, especially on cold nights when conversation and laughter would have warmed her as much as the fire.

A heavy sigh escaped the woman's lips as she returned to her sewing and listened to the sound of the air whistling by. Her homeland was a quiet place. Once, a king ruled, and there were castles and noble lords and ladies, but a curse had befallen the land, and the king left on a quest to uncover a way to remove it.

As time passed, the crops dwindled but didn't die. Livestock survived but grew lean. No one in the land seemed to be able to grow or keep more food than they could use for themselves. Trading with outside kingdoms stopped, and anyone who wanted to become rich or simply live a comfortable life moved from their homes. When the king left, others tried to rule but departed after they could not obtain taxes from the few, poor remaining dwellers. Invading armies starved when they came with plans of conquest. It was only a couple of years before everyone left them alone. Fewer and fewer people lived in the cursed kingdom, and soon, it would be forgotten with just a few like herself able to grow enough food to survive.

She sighed again, her thoughts miserable tonight, when combined with the wind and the cold. Perhaps she should leave, too; move to a nearby village in the next kingdom over, perhaps marry a good man and start a family. She stared into the fire, pondering these thoughts, when she heard a sound she didn't recognize at first: knocking on her door. The sound was weak but urgent, and she rushed to the door and opened it.

A stranger stood in her doorway. The man was old and withered and looked as if he might fall to the floor at any moment. She helped him inside and laid him on her bed near the fire. He mumbled incoherently and shivered as she took off his wet clothes and wrapped him in blankets to warm him. She immediately recognized the signs of fever and ladled the small remains of stew she'd had for dinner into a bowl. Gently, she held the man's head up and helped him eat. He took no more than four bites of the stew before closing his eyes and falling into a deep slumber. She put the bowl near the hearth, placed three logs in the embers, then made herself comfortable on the floor in front of the fireplace. After some time, the woman closed her eyes and slept, her last thoughts swirling about the stranger asleep a few feet away.

Chapter One

Princess Rose sat on the steps of the royal dais among the dresses, jewels, draperies, and shoes that were her birthday presents. Her head was slightly cocked to one side, her blonde hair spilling over one delicate shoulder, catching the late morning sunlight which was cascading across the courtyard. Her slender face bore a look of curiosity as she studied a colorful map in front of her.

Now, Rose knew what the markings on the map meant; her mother had insisted she be taught about them once she was old enough to read. As much as Rose enjoyed maps, she was puzzled as to why it had been given to her on her thirteenth birthday—the first day of her womanhood. Her younger sisters—Tulip, Blossom, Daisy, and Violet—sat around her, silently admiring her gift, though, Daisy could not help but fidget, as was her nature.

"Why, thank you," the princess said as she looked at the guests for the grateful face of the unknown giver. Each person regarded the other, but no one responded.

"Well, I say, that looks to be very interesting," said King Charles, which was his response to every gift Rose had received that day. He leaned forward in his throne and held out his hand for the map. Rose bowed to her father and gracefully passed it to him. The king sat back and stroked his beard as he gave the map his full regard. "Yes, yes. Very...," the king turned the map right side up, "...interesting."

A hearty laugh rippled through the group of royal guests. King Charles was known for joking often in close company, and the kingdom loved him for it. Of all the royals of the known kingdoms, His Highness of Ametheria was regarded as the most at ease with himself.

Queen Isabel gave a polite smile in response to her husband's foolishness. "My dear, you know your head is for swords and horses, not maps. May I?"

The map now passed from king to queen with a smirk and a shrug from His Highness causing more laughter from the guests. Queen Isabel sat straight in her throne as her dark eyes glanced briefly at the map. Aside from the color of her eyes and hair, the queen looked very much like Rose. With a slight nod, she rolled up the map.

"A fine gift. Very thoughtful," she said and handed the map to her chambermaid with a whisper.

Rose watched as she did this and realized that, perhaps, for the first time in her life, she had just seen her mother troubled.

The party went on as most royal parties did with a feast, dancing, carnival games, a gypsy parade, and horseback riding. Rose danced with her sisters as the royal court musicians played a festive tune. Dancing was not Rose's finest skill, something her sister Blossom often took pleasure in pointing out to her, but she laughed as she made her way zigzagging between her sisters until, inevitably, she collided with the youngest, knocking her to the ground.

"Oh, Violet!" Rose cried as she helped her sister to her feet. "Forgive me!"

Rose fretted about the girl looking for any injury. Violet was tiny for her age and appeared as fragile as an eggshell.

"Did you knock over the 'Little Sparrow,' again, Rose?" Blossom asked with a smirk. "I would wager you will break at least one of her legs by the time we get to your fifteenth birthday festival."

Rose scowled at her sister's sharp tongue, but Violet, ever the gentle soul, said softly to her oldest sister, "I am not hurt. Do not be upset."

Rose patted her sister on the head with a smile and kissed it. "Your patience could fill the oceans beyond the horizon." She then leaned close with a sly smirk and glanced around as if someone might spy. "How about you sneak us a sweet roll from the baker's tent?"

Violet's eyes narrowed and she, too, looked about. Being small did have advantages and, less than a minute later, she and Rose sat on the grass, sharing a pastry dripping with colorful swirls of icing, and laughing together.

As fond as Rose was of carnival treats and games, she took the most pleasure from riding her prized horse, Wisher, for the entertainment of their guests. Her father held Rose as the best rider in the kingdom and often had her demonstrate her skills to others.

As Rose walked to the courtyard, she could see Wisher already waiting inside the fence. The horse's golden coat and mane had been freshly brushed, making their sheen nearly identical to that of Rose's blonde locks. Joseph, her royal stable boy, stood next to Wisher. Rose had befriended Joseph years ago during her riding lessons and felt as close to him as she would a brother. The lean fifteen-year-old lad patted the horse lightly and guided the horse toward the approaching princess.

"Good afternoon, Princess Rose of Ametheria," Joseph said with a bow.

Rose blushed. "Here, now. What is this formality, Joseph?"

"You are a woman now, and I am humbled to be in your presence," Joseph said, bowing deeper.

Rose slapped the top of Joseph's head and looked about. "Stop it. You will have the Duchess of Lenstein spreading gossip, and my mother shall have to go to war over it."

Joseph stood. "By 'going to war,' you mean, sending His Highness the King to the Duke's manor and drinking the night away? That is a war I would like to start." The two friends laughed for a moment as Wisher stood by patiently. Joseph stepped to the horse's side and offered his knee to the princess. "Your horse, Princess," he said.

Rose placed a foot on Joseph's knee, took his hand, and deftly swung up onto Wisher's back. She carefully adjusted her riding habit and took the reigns as Joseph stepped away. When she was at the ready, she patted Wisher on the side and said, as she always did, "Run free, Wisher, and carry me with you."

The party came to a standstill as Rose and Wisher began their ride around the field. If a horse had been born for a rider,

Wisher had been born for Rose. King Charles stood from his chair and strode to the fence to watch his daughter perform.

Rose and Wisher trotted around the fence line once. After the lap, Rose patted Wisher, and the horse began a gallop to the center of the yard where two of the queen's royal guard stood. As Rose rode toward the first guard, he knelt and held out a sheathed sword. The horse did not break stride as Rose swung herself gracefully over the saddle, grabbed the handle, and unsheathed the sword as she rode past.

The party members applauded as Rose straightened in the saddle and rode toward the second guard. Rose whistled, and the guard tossed an apple into the air. Rose's sword glinted in the midday sun as she sliced the fruit in half. As the applause grew louder, Wisher approached a wooden target. Rose hefted the sword over her shoulder, aimed, and let it fly. Cheers erupted as the blade sunk into the center of the painted circle.

King Charles beamed and clapped as Rose trotted over to him and gave the reigns a slight tug. Wisher halted and bowed his head at the king.

"My eldest daughter!" the king announced. The partiers applauded again. The king called for his horse, and his stable boy set off to fetch it.

But Rose was not watching her father or listening to the applause. Her attention was fixed on something happening in the farthest corner of the party.

Queen Isabel led Joseph behind a carnival tent, both deep in a private conversation. As they started to step behind the cloth, Joseph turned and regarded Rose with what appeared to her to be worried eyes. He then turned away and disappeared behind the tent.

Rose and her sisters, dressed in their bedclothes and robes, entered their parents' chambers as they prepared to turn in for the night. Queen Isabel and King Charles placed the cards they had been playing face down on the table as their children stood in a line from youngest to oldest.

"We have come to bid you goodnight, Your Highness," the littlest said.

"And goodnight to you, My Precious," said the queen as she held out her arms. The six-year-old ran over and squeezed her mother tightly. "Oh, you will be a handful tonight, will you not?" the mother said with a light laugh. Violet giggled and joined her sisters. One by one, each daughter hugged her mother goodnight until it was Rose's turn.

Rose approached her mother but hesitated.

"Why, dear, what is the matter?" asked the Queen.

"Mother," Rose looked closely for the trouble she had seen brewing earlier in the queen's eyes. Now, she could find none. "Does a Lady still hug her mother, the Queen, or do I now curtsey?"

The Queen smiled. "A Lady always hugs her mother, especially one who loves her daughter so."

Rose embraced her mother, and all her fears and worries from the day vanished. "I could never have dreamed of a finer mother than you," she whispered. When Rose pulled away, she saw tears in the Queen's eyes. Rose gave a curtsey to her father then joined her sisters.

King Charles took his wife's hand as she dabbed her eyes. "Nevermore has there been such a blessed family as the one in this room," he said.

Isabel looked at the princesses. "Now, what do we say, my children?"

In unison, the sisters said, "Tomorrow is another shining day in the land of Ametheria, and we must do our best to be kind and good to all we meet."

"Always remember that, my darlings. Especially you, Rose," the queen said.

Rose, momentarily surprised by her mother's interjection, bowed. The five princesses turned and left the chamber, closing the door behind them.

In the hall leading to the bedchambers, the princesses walked in silence. As each sister reached her chamber, she curtseyed to the remaining princesses and entered. Inside each chamber was a waiting chambermaid, ready to tuck her in. Soon, the two eldest princesses, Rose and Tulip, were left alone walking in the hall.

"Tulip, what do you think Mother meant by that last remark?" Rose asked.

Tulip contemplated for a moment. Rose had always found Tulip's extraordinary intelligence helpful, especially when it came to figuring out the thoughts or behavior of others. "I suppose, as a woman, you must be more courteous than we children are expected to be."

Rose nodded. It was as good an answer as she could come up with, and in keeping with the spirit of the day, it made sense. But then, as Tulip reached for the latch on her chamber door, she turned and looked at her sister in a frightful seriousness.

"Mother is not herself today," said Tulip, "and I am not sure why."

Without another word or chance for Rose to respond, Tulip entered her room and closed the door.

Rose stood motionless in the hall. The air had a chill she had not noticed before, and she clutched her robe tightly to her breast. This was the first night Rose would be without a chambermaid, and she now felt isolated and alone.

Silly goose. You are too old for childish fears.

Rose approached her chamber and went inside. She removed her robe, sat on the edge of her bed, and drank the cup of tea her parents always left for each daughter at bedtime. She noticed the tea had an unusual flavor to it that evening, and it had an odor much like fermented fruit, but as a dutiful princess, she drank the rest with no waste and settled in for her first night's sleep as a woman. She gazed out her window at the dark clouds drifting over the moon. Crickets in the grass far below seemed to sing a soothing lullaby as Rose's lids grew heavy and closed in a deep sleep.

Chapter Two

Rose's eyes squinted against the glare of the morning sun streaming in from the window. She stretched on the bed and yawned as her eyelids fluttered open. As sleep left her body, she sensed something different about her room. After a moment, she realized, with surprise, that it wasn't even her room at all.

Rose sat upright, and the sudden rush of movement caused the room to sway before her eyes and her head to ache.

I must speak with the kitchen staff about that tea. It was obviously bad.

She squeezed her eyes shut until the swaying feeling passed. Slowly, she opened her eyes and looked around. She was lying on a small but comfortable bed in what appeared to be a one-room cottage she had never seen before. On one side of the cottage was a dresser with two supply packs leaning against it. On the other side of the cottage was a table set for a breakfast of steak, eggs, and bread. In the center of the table was a silver tray, and in the center of the silver tray was a rolled-up parchment.

Rose spied her robe draped at the foot of the bed, and she quickly put it on over her bedclothes. She pulled herself out of bed carefully—her legs experiencing a strange, weakened feeling—and tied the robe tightly.

"Hello?" she called.

There was no answer.

As strength returned to her body, Rose searched what little space there was in the cottage for any signs of life. Finding no one, she pulled open the door and stepped outside. The cottage stood in the center of a forest with a single path from the doorway that disappeared into the trees. Rose hurried around the cottage, looking for any sign of where she was or how to return to the palace. The forest looked no different than any of the ones she and her royal guards rode through on summer days but offered no clue as to which direction her home was located. Fear crept into the princess's heart as she hurried back to the entrance of the cottage. She opened her mouth to call out for aid, then she stopped short.

From somewhere in the forest, footsteps approached.

Rose looked down the path, seeing no one. Whoever was coming, they were making their way through the trees. Quietly, Rose backed into the cabin and closed the door. She listened as the person drew nearer to the cabin. Looking around for protection, Rose quickly picked up a knife from the table and hid it away in the fold of her robe as the latch on the cottage door raised. The door swung open.

"Joseph! Oh, thank heavens!" Rose walked over and pulled the stable boy in.

"Good morning, Princess," Joseph said as he sat a pitcher of milk down on the table. He slid a goblet toward her and began to pour. "My apologies if I startled you, but I needed to fetch the milk for breakfast before we set out—" Suddenly, Joseph turned his eyes away. "Your Highness, forgive me," he said. "I thought you would have dressed by now. I will take my leave until you are ready for company."

Rose stepped between Joseph and the door. "You will not go anywhere until you tell me what is going on, Joseph," she said, her brows furrowed and eyes blazing. "Who brought me here and why?"

Joseph looked at the princess with a cocked eyebrow. He then glanced at the parchment still rolled on the table. "Ah, you haven't read that yet."

Rose shook her head.

Joseph pulled out the chair from the breakfast table and walked to the front door, placing a hand on Rose's shoulder. "When you are ready, I will be waiting outside." He smiled, then stepped outside and closed the door.

Rose walked over to the table, sat down and picked up the parchment. The roll contained several pages and was held together by a wax seal. Stamped in the wax was her family crest. Rose broke the seal and hurriedly unrolled the pages. As she did so, she immediately recognized her mother's handwriting as she read.

Dearest Rose,

Please forgive me for the circumstances you have been placed in, but it is required for the journey on which you are about to partake. Since your birth, I and your father have known this day was to come. Alas, we could not imagine it was to be this soon.

But I must start at the beginning. Many generations ago, this land, our home, was ravaged with a curse. Blight had befallen the land, and the ruling king left seeking a remedy but had not returned. Then, one day, a strange man arrived. He appeared without wealth and seemed on the verge of death as he journeyed from home to home seeking shelter. It was a kindly woman of sixteen who eventually brought the man into her home, sharing with him her meager dinner, and gave him her bed as she slept by the hearth. It was not until the morning that the man spoke his first words.

"My dear," said he, "you truly are kind of spirit and good of heart. It takes strength to be as such in these times."

The woman told him to be still and rest, but he would not remain silent. "No, my dear. My time is at hand, as it should be for one as old as I—older than you might believe.

"I am the king of this land, who left many years ago to find the answer to what ails the kingdom, but I am more than that, as well. I am, or I was, a powerful wizard, who founded this kingdom as a place of love and light. I wished to make a happy place of peace where all could prosper, but as years and years passed, I grew lazy and greedy. And so, the magic I worked on this land began to work against me and the people here. I left to find an answer, and after much searching, I know that you are the answer I sought."

He then motioned to the small bag he had been carrying and she handed it to the man, who pulled out a worn map, much like the one you received yesterday. He held it out and asked her to take it. She grasped one end of the roll as he held the other. As the man spoke, the woman could feel something she would later describe as a warm light pass from the man, through the map, and into her.

15

"When I am gone, this parchment will be all that remains of who I was," he said. "You must follow it to the beginning of your journey. Once there, it will serve you no more. You must then continue until the journey is at its end. If you succeed, you will be blessed with a homeland free of its curse and full of richness and peace that you shall rule over. You shall also be blessed with children beautiful in spirit and body. But these blessings must always be earned. Every firstborn daughter of the royal bloodline henceforth will receive this parchment when they are ready to take their own journey. And, none of these daughters must know of the journeys prior, for their knowledge of travels past may affect their travels future. When they return, they will be the new ruler of this land."

The sorcerer released the parchment and lay back on the bed, very weak. He closed his eyes and spoke his last words:

"Tomorrow will be a shining day in the land of Ametheria. Do your best to be kind and good to all those you meet."

The woman, your Great-Great-Great-Great-Great Grand-mother Elsbeth, cried as the man's spirit passed on. To her astonishment, his body shimmered in a golden light and vanished from her bed. The only remnant of his existence was the map she held in her hand.

And so, the woman who would be known as Queen Elsbeth of Ametheria set off on her journey. Several years and many adventures later, she returned. Her wisdom guided the people of the land, and by the time of her marriage to your ancestor, King Consort Eldric, Ametheria was enjoying its first joyous year.

And now you know of the purpose of the map you have before you. You are the youngest to have ever received the map, and for that, I have great fear. But to deny the journey is to risk *darkness befalling the people of Ametheria, and as Queen, I cannot allow that to happen and must have faith in you to partake this hardship now. But you shall not have to take it alone.*

Many times, a companion has been chosen to accompany the princess on her journey. I and your father have chosen Joseph for this task. This choice was made for many reasons but mostly for his deep loyalty to you and your trust in him. Have faith in these two things, for they will be a help and comfort for you.

Know that no matter where your quest leads you, no matter how far you are from home, I am always there with you. I love you. Be good and kind to all those you meet.

Your Mother

Rose placed the pages on the table as emotions swirled within her. She stood from the chair, approached the dresser, and looked inside. Instead of the dresses or gowns she was accustomed to, the clothes of a common girl lay within. She dressed and went to the front door.

Joseph sat waiting in the grass beside the path. He looked up at Rose with a smile and offered her a newly-picked buttercup. Rose walked over and sat next to him, taking the flower.

"So, how long have you known of this?" Rose asked as she looked at the flower.

"Since I turned thirteen, Princess," Joseph replied. "I wished to tell you many times, but your mother, the Queen, was adamant—and rightly so—that you should not be burdened with knowing until the map arrived."

Rose gazed at the delicate yellow flower in her hand. She turned and regarded Joseph for a moment, considering all she had just learned about the person she knew as a friend. She then tickled his nose with the buttercup.

"I think we had better eat our fill," she said. "We apparently have a long journey ahead of us."

A half-hour later, the breakfast plates were empty, and Joseph and Rose sat hunched over the map. Using her knife, she guided Joseph along the markings.

"See here? This is the cottage," Rose explained. "The small line is the path leading away from here and to a road. You have seen that, I take it?"

"No, Princess," Joseph replied. "I was sent here through another path, hidden in the forest, shown to me by the Queen yesterday. I do not know what lies beyond the path leading from the door."

"Very well," said Rose. "We follow the road until we come to a small river settlement. Once there, we must ferry across and travel due east until we come to a single building standing by the road. It appears that building is our destination."

"Why do you say that?" asked Joseph.

Rose pointed to a small cross by the marking of the building. "See there? That means there is something by the road in front of the building. I think whatever that is will contain the information we need to begin our quest."

Joseph stretched and gathered the two supply packs. With a heave, he hoisted them onto his back. "Then, I suppose we had better be on our way."

"Hold," the princess said with authority. "I will carry my pack, if you will."

"Your Highness, a princess—"

"Is not travelling with you," Rose said. "I am not dressed in my royal robes, and I do not carry the royal seal of Ametheria.

I think this is for disguise, and you shall abide by that. Am I understood?"

"But Princess—"

"And that is another thing," Rose interrupted. "No more of this 'Princess' or 'Your Highness' nonsense. You will refer to me as 'Rose' until this journey is at an end."

Joseph's face flushed and after a moment, he said, "If you insist, Rose." He set one of the packs on the floor, and Rose slung it over her shoulder. Joseph, with eyes turned low, walked past Rose and started to open the door.

"Joseph," Rose said. Joseph turned and looked at the kind eyes of his friend. "I am glad it is you with me."

And, with that, they left.

Chapter Three

It was not until midday when Rose and Joseph spied the road crossing ahead of the tree-lined path. With a sigh of relief, Joseph paused a moment as he set his pack down.

"We should keep moving if we are to make the river settlement by nightfall," Rose said.

"We shall not make the settlement until tomorrow, at least," Joseph replied as he took a seat on a toppled tree. "We can take a moment to rest."

Rose did not say a word as she placed her pack on the ground and sat in the middle of the path. Joseph produced a knife and an apple from his pack and cut into it. He put a slice in his mouth and offered another to Rose. Taking the slice, she sucked on the juice and looked around the forest as the sun peeked through the dense branches above. Rose was certain she was not far from the palace. She tried her best to guess the direction of the setting sun to see if she could figure out the way home.

"Tell me if I am correct, Joseph," Rose said as she traced a line through the air with her finger. "Home should be…that way."

Rose pointed in a direction though the trees as a shape suddenly moved near them. Rose paused, unsure if what she had just seen was a trick of the shadows. After a moment, another movement caught her eye.

"Joseph," Rose whispered.

"I know," Joseph replied as he cut another slice of apple. "I figured the smell would bring him out sooner or later. I am a bit surprised he did not find us sooner."

The loud snap of a branch under a heavy step shot out from the forest, and Rose immediately was on her feet. "Who is it?"

Joseph tossed a large apple slice onto the middle of the path. Something pushed through the trees, and the mysterious creature stepped into view.

"Wisher!" Rose exclaimed as she ran to her horse. Wisher nuzzled Rose and bent down to take the apple slice as the princess hugged him. On Wisher's back was a modest double rider saddle and reins. Joseph patted Wisher as he slung their packs over the horse's back. He then held out his hand and helped Rose up into the front seat of the saddle.

"So, what do you say? Do you think we will make the settlement by supper?" Joseph asked as he mounted the seat behind her.

"With enough time for dessert, I imagine," Rose replied.

———————————

It was early on the third day, after leaving the river town, that their destination came into view.

"Joseph, look!" Rose exclaimed.

Ahead of them sat an abandoned, two-story cottage by the road with a post in front for tying horses. When they reached the cottage, Rose and Joseph dismounted Wisher and tied him to the post. Joseph approached the front door as Rose pulled the map from her pouch. Joseph knocked on the door, but no one answered. He tried to lift the latch, but it would not budge.

"There appears to be no one home, if anyone still lives here," Joseph said as he walked back to Rose, who had taken a seat on a tree stump, examining the map. A small, grey kitten rubbed against her legs as she studied, and she scratched the kitten's head.

"Good kitty. Go on home, now," she said as she gave the kitten a light pat. The kitten walked away from Rose and sat near the house, cleaning itself.

Joseph knelt next to Rose. "Any ideas?"

"I think what we need is somewhere in front of the house, not inside it," she said. "I know the cross on the map means something. I just don't know what."

"An object?" asked Joseph.

"Yes," Rose replied. "Maybe the stump I am sitting on." Rose stood, rolling up the map, and she and Joseph examined the tree stump looking for markings, secret compartments, or even a passage underneath. They decided the stump held no meaning.

"Maybe the cross is us," Joseph suggested. "Maybe we are to wait for whatever is to come."

Rose began to unroll the map yet again but thought better of it. There was nothing there she had not seen already. "You may be right. Let us give it some time." She placed the map back in her supply bag.

Noon passed. Rose and Joseph spent much of the day looking around the cottage, playing dice, or simply waiting. Night fell, and eventually morning broke. When noon arrived again and nothing had happened, Rose decided to look at the map again. She unrolled it and looked at the markings. She blinked her eyes and stared down unbelievingly.

The cross was gone.

Rose called Joseph over and he verified what she saw.

"Did it rub away, you think?" he asked.

Rose shook her head. "It is as if it was never there to begin with." She concentrated on the symbol of the cottage on the map as if trying to make the cross reappear. She caught a slight movement from the corner of her eye, and, thinking it was a fly or dust speck, she brushed her hand across the map. Rose stopped suddenly and stared. She blinked her eyes again and looked closer.

The cross was on a different part of the map.

"It has moved!" Rose said with surprise and excitement. "Joseph, look!"

Now, it was Joseph's turn to blink his eyes, not believing what he saw. The small cross on the map was now at a point farther up the road away from the cottage. He stared harder and, in a whisper, said, "Rose, I may be mistaken, but I think I see it actually moving."

Rose and Joseph placed the map on the tree stump and studied it. After twenty minutes, it was obvious the marking had indeed moved farther along the road on the map. Rose quickly did some figuring in her mind.

"It is a person, not on horseback. He is moving too slow," she said. Without hesitation, she scooped up the map, untied Wisher, and was on his back in a moment, with Joseph quickly following.

"It is not that far," she said. A quick snap of the reins, and the horse galloped down the road.

Rose pulled on the reigns, easing Wisher to a halt. She looked along the empty road with a mixture of puzzlement and frustration. The road ahead was empty, and she was sure they had passed no one since they left the cottage. Quickly, Joseph removed the map, and they looked for the cross mark. Rose became fully frustrated when she saw they were well beyond the cross marking on the map.

Rose clicked her tongue and pulled on Wisher's reigns, turning the horse around. She stared down the road they had just traveled, trying to see anything that would make sense of the marking on the map. There was nothing.

"Perhaps if we try again at a slower pace?" Joseph suggested.

Rose shook her head. "Whatever it is, it is still heading this way. Let us have lunch by the roadside, and we will see what comes."

And so, the two friends guided Wisher to the wooded side of the road and tied him to a nearby tree. Rose produced bread, cheeses, salt-cured pork, and cider from her pack. Joseph joined her by the roadside, and they ate, each of them keeping their eyes on the road.

A half-hour passed, when Joseph spotted something. Silently, he tapped Rose on the shoulder and pointed. Rose looked up. Peering out at them from a small area of brush was the grey kitten from the cottage. Rose took the map from her pack and studied it. The cross mark was, to the best of her knowledge, right on the spot where they lunched.

Rose placed the map back and got to her feet. Upon her movement, the kitten quickly pulled its head back into the shadows of the brush.

"It is okay, kitty," Rose said in a soft voice. "Here, here. We will not hurt you."

The kitten remained in its hiding spot. Rose produced a tiny morsel of cheese and held it out to the kitten. After a minute, the kitten crept out of its hiding spot and made its way cautiously to the princess. It sniffed at the cheese and began to nibble on it.

"There you go, little one," Rose said. She gently stroked the kitten's back as it ate. She could feel the kitten's ribs under her fingers. "Oh, my, you are starved. Poor kitty," she said. Rose placed more cheese on the ground as the kitten continued eating. She then took shreds of pork and pinches of bread and placed them on the ground. Rose and Joseph remained silent as the kitten gobbled up the meal. Afterward, the kitten sat and washed the salt from its paws.

Rose watched the animal. Speaking mostly to herself, Rose wondered aloud, "So, are you what I am supposed to find?"

The kitten stopped cleaning, looked up and said, "Dear Princess, who else?"

Rose and Joseph sat in stunned silence. "A little bit of a surprise, am I not?" the kitten asked.

Rose finally found her voice. "Indeed," she said. "I apologize if I seem, well, out-of-sorts, but you are the first creature I have ever encountered that…can *speak*."

"If it comforts you, I am the first creature I have ever heard talk, myself," the kitten said. Joseph cleared his throat. "Kitten, do you know why we have come here?"

The kitten regarded Joseph for a moment. "Ah…dear sir, I am most sorry, but I cannot seem to answer your question. Oh, I would most be happy to, but I just cannot seem to."

"What about I?" asked Rose. "If I asked you if you knew why we were here…"

"Ah! Then, I would say, yes!" exclaimed the kitten.

Joseph looked at Rose. "It is your journey. It appears you must be the one to do all the tasks at hand."

Rose reached down and scooped the kitten up. "Hey, now. Easy does it," the kitten exclaimed. Rose gently scratched the kitten's ears, and a purr rumbled from the little creature.

"Ooooooh, I like her," the kitten said to Joseph. He and Rose laughed as the kitten stretched in her grasp and relaxed.

"Dear kitten, do you have a name?" Rose asked.

The kitten continued to purr. "No name. No owner, no name."

"Then you shall be Snowflake, little grey one," said the princess. This met with more happy purrs.

"Snowflake?" asked Joseph.

"Hush," Rose playfully scolded. "My quest. My kitten."

Rose placed Snowflake on the ground. The kitten stretched as Rose and Joseph looked at each other. It was time to find out what was ahead of them.

"Snowflake," Rose asked, "what is my journey?"

Snowflake looked up at his new owner; to Rose it looked as if his eyes contained sympathy for her. "My dear princess," he began, "you are to travel a great distance. There are many strange, wondrous sights to see and many dangers to face. You are seeking something that is in several pieces. It is your coronation gown, princess. It is said the gown was spun by an Elfish tailor from gold found in the well of a volcano. The gown is in four pieces and hidden in locations far and wide. The first piece you shall seek is the skirt. The second is the blouse. The third are the slippers. The fourth and final piece is your crown. I only know of the location of one of the pieces: your skirt. It is located high upon the peak of Jagged Mountain in the kingdom of Merc. There, you must obtain the first piece of your coronation gown."

The kitten was quiet. Rose and Joseph looked at each other, both familiar with the name of Merc. And both were familiar with how distant the kingdom was.

"Snowflake," she asked, "how long will it take to reach the mountain peak?"

"Four months. Maybe just under a half-year, princess," he answered.

Rose stood and stepped away from the others, her back toward them. "How long will I be away from home?"

"All I can tell you is that you will not be the age you are now, princess," Snowflake said.

Joseph rose to his feet but a slight wave from the princess stopped him in his place. She turned toward them with a look of resolve.

"I guess we had better begin, then," she said.

Chapter Four

Winters were harsh in the Kingdom of Merc. Ice storms were more common than snow, and the people of the kingdom were regarded as the sturdiest people in any land. Due to their dependence on each other to survive such seasons, all people who crossed their lands were given any help needed and Rose and Joseph enjoyed every consideration as they made their way toward the looming mountain at the edge of the kingdom.

Three separate times, the trio found themselves stranded in the home of kind people. On one of those occasions, they remained icebound with a family for five weeks. During that time, Joseph worked for the father, who was a blacksmith, and Rose tutored the house's seven children on proper handwriting and painting. In return, the mother taught Rose her cooking skills and the princess delighted in crafting her own food, even if most of the dishes contained turnips and radishes—two of Merc's primary crops.

Snowflake provided another source of happiness. The kitten did not speak around anyone, but the children seemed to delight in playing with him. Rose noticed Snowflake did not care to be in the presence of the family's baby, who pulled his tail constantly. When it was time for the travelers to leave, there were many tears from everyone, though the father tried to hide his.

Several weeks later, the spring sun graced the kingdom, and Rose and Joseph found themselves nearing the mountain peak. Thanks to the generosity of the people of Merc, they were never short of supplies during their difficult trek.

As the trio continued up the mountain, the journey became more and more dangerous, and Rose and Joseph found it easier to lead Wisher through the ever-narrowing path, rather than ride him.

On a morning heavy with fog, Rose paused as she spied something ahead of them just off the mountain path. Hanging between distant edges of a deep crevice in the mountain was a rope bridge. The bridge looked quite old but well-made and sturdy. It had the classic design of a footbridge, but was unusually wide. The thick ropes weaving through it seemed strong and there appeared to be no boards loose or missing. A low cloud hung over the distant end of the bridge, concealing where it led from sight.

Rose tied Wisher to a lone standing tree. She took one of the support ropes in her hand and shook it. It had little sway and seemed safe enough. She put a foot on the first board, and Joseph rested a hand on her shoulder.

"Allow me to go first and find out what awaits us on the other side," he said.

"This is my journey, remember?" Rose said as she began to turn back toward the bridge, but Joseph held fast.

"And you will continue it after I see what is over there," he said. "Please."

Rose locked eyes with Joseph in a silent challenge to see who would back down first.

"Ah, Princess?" Snowflake said. "Perhaps the lad is right on this."

"You said *I* would face many great dangers," Rose said not taking her eyes from Joseph's.

"And you shall, Your Highness," the cat said. "But not unnecessarily. Your trials are to come, I am sure, but there is no harm in the good man having a simple look-see, is there?"

Rose stood her ground for a minute more, then, slowly and deliberately, she stepped aside from the mouth of the bridge. Without a word, Joseph walked onto the bridge. He held one of the support ropes as he journeyed further and further. As he reached the middle of the bridge, he stopped.

Rose looked at Joseph so far off in the distance. She wasn't sure, but it seemed as if he was listening to something. Then, he looked at the boards beneath his feet.

"Joseph?" Rose called, a touch of worry escaping her throat. "Joseph, what is it?"

Joseph looked back at Rose. There was an expression of something Rose had never seen in Joseph's features before: fear. Suddenly, the boards underneath Joseph's feet began to shake. Joseph clutched a support rope as one foot slipped over the edge.

"Joseph!" Rose cried as she raced onto the bridge.

"No! Do not come out here, Rose!" Joseph called as he held tight onto the ropes. Rose never broke stride as Joseph continued to plead to her. "Rose, go back! Hurry!"

As Rose neared her friend, she could see more of his leg hanging over the side of the bridge. At first, she thought a stray rope had wound itself around his ankle, but as she closed the gap between her and Joseph, she could see it was not a rope at all.

"Rose, run!" Joseph screamed. "There is something under the bridge!"

A large, dark arm snaked out from under the boards and clutched Joseph's leg. Rose stood motionless for a moment as her mind tried to accept what she saw. As she and Joseph stood on the bridge, hundreds of meters above the ground, another arm appeared from under the bridge and clamped onto one of the boards. Rose grabbed a support rope to keep from tumbling over the side as something pulled itself up and into the middle of the bridge between her and Joseph.

The troll was almost twice the size of Joseph. Knotted, brambly fur covered its thick, strong frame. Rose could not see the monster's eyes from under the ridge of its massive brow, but the long, jagged teeth that hung from its mouth were in full view.

The troll reached out to Rose with long, sharp fingers as she tried to back away from the advancing creature. Her foot stepped beyond the side of the bridge and, with a shriek, Rose tumbled downward, slipping between the ropes as she grasped for them. The world spun wildly around her as she fell. Suddenly, she felt her arm caught in the powerful grip of the troll. It peered down at her as she hung in the open air. With no

31

effort, the creature pulled Rose up to it and carried her as it tromped toward the end of the bridge.

Snowflake arched his spine and backed away as the troll exited the bridge and placed Rose on the ground. Rose scooted a few feet away from the troll as it advanced a step toward her. With its thick mouth, the troll said, "You will not cross my bridge."

Rushing footsteps approached from the bridge, and before anyone could react, Joseph sprung in the air just behind the troll's head. Joseph planted his feet on top of the troll's furry shoulders and pushed himself off, sending the troll stumbling backward. Joseph twisted in the air and landed nimbly on his feet between Rose and the creature.

The troll caught itself against the bridge posts and shook off Joseph's surprise attack. Its lips curled back as it grabbed at a rock the size of a calf with one of its thick hands and charged toward Joseph and Rose. Before the troll could overrun them, Joseph fell back on top of Rose and rolled them both out of the way. The troll tripped over its clawed feet and fell facedown on the jagged cliff side.

In an instant, Joseph was on his feet again. "Wait here," he said to Rose then strode toward the rising troll.

The troll groaned as he stood. Joseph stopped in front of him and looked upward at his shaken and angered opponent. "We need to cross that bridge," he said. "Are you going to yield?"

The troll stood for a moment, visibly thinking over its options. It suddenly swung its arm at Joseph as if to swat him from sight. Rose and Snowflake watched in mutual astonishment as Joseph easily avoided the blow and grabbed onto the creature's outstretched arm. Using the momentum of the troll's swing, Joseph pulled himself up and around to the back of the hairy beast and bent the large arm behind it. The troll bellowed in surprise as Joseph then drove the heel of his foot into the troll's leg at the bend of the knee, sending the giant toppling to the earth, facedown for the second time.

Rose approached Joseph and the monster he had pinned beneath him. The troll snorted and shouted in angry bursts but, try as it might, it could not roll Joseph off him.

"Fools! Imbeciles!" the troll shouted. "I will stomp you all if you do not leave now!"

Joseph held fast. "I think not, troll," he said. "You are defeated and must yield. We must cross that bridge, and you are standing in our way."

The troll grew still and silent. For many moments, Joseph and Rose waited to see the troll's response, but none came. Then, quietly, the troll began to make a sound. Neither Joseph nor Rose could make out what the troll was doing or saying. Finally, Rose knelt toward its downturned face.

"Rose, I would not do that," Joseph said, but having the troll pinned, he could not make any move to stop her. The moment he relaxed, the troll could toss him in the air like a pebble.

Rose bent down to look at the face of the monster they had defeated. What she saw brought a sudden, soft cry to her lips. The troll was sobbing; its eyes dripping tears to the ground below.

"Joseph, let him up," Rose said.

Joseph looked at the princess. "That is not...," he began but stopped. There was no question in Rose's eyes. Joseph took a deep breath, steeled his tiring body, and leaped away from the troll, pulling Rose back with him.

The troll remained lying face down on the ground. Slowly, it pulled in its legs under it and sat up on its knees. Joseph and

Rose looked at the troll's face for what seemed like the very first time. Imbedded in the cruel, cracked features, were two shimmering, blue eyes, like two spring pools. The troll looked away in shame, wiped the wetness from its face, and sat back against a boulder.

"You may do as you wish," the troll said, keeping its face turned away. "The path is clear."

Rose did not hesitate. She approached the troll and placed a hand on its shoulder. She withheld a shudder as she felt the matted, filthy fur under her palm, but the kindness in her eyes never left.

"Troll, look at me," she said. "Please."

After a moment, the troll did as the princess asked.

"What is your name?" Rose asked.

"Brute," it said. "I carry the name of my father, though I am not as big as he was."

"You are big to me, Brute," Rose said. She saw a large scrape above the troll's left eye from where he had fallen on the ground. "I am sorry we hurt you. It was not intentional."

"I would like to hear the young lad say that," Brute said as he jabbed an accusing thumb at Joseph. Joseph rolled his eyes and turned away.

"He was protecting a friend," Rose said. "Here, let me tend to your forehead."

Brute took Rose's hand in his and patted it. "There is no need," he said. "I have had worse. Besides, I got this tripping over my clumsy feet, nothing more."

Brute stood and arched his back. A sound like a tree breaking in half shot from his spine, and he let roll a long, loud sigh of relief.

"That is better," he said as his shoulders slumped in relaxation. "I had been hanging under that bridge for the better part of the day. You three sure took your time getting here."

"You mean you knew we were coming?" Joseph asked.

"Well, yes, at least, since this morning," Brute responded. "My eyes may not be much use in the morning mist, but I could hear you coming up the mountainside since just after daybreak."

"Those are some mighty sharp ears you have, then," said Snowflake. "Your hearing is likely better than mine."

Brute remained silent for a moment. Then, the massive troll, with wide eyes, turned to Rose.

"That cat can *talk*!" he exclaimed.

Rose and Joseph suddenly burst into laughter as Snowflake and Brute stood looking at them with puzzled expressions.

Brute held Snowflake in one massive hand as the cat told them of their journey across the kingdom at the bottom of the mountain, while Rose assisted Joseph in wrapping a bandage around his strained arms.

"You need to wrap just a little tighter around that arm, Rose," Joseph said. "That one is the weakest from having to hold Brute's arm behind him."

"About that, Joseph," said Rose, "where did you learn to fight in such a manner?"

"Promise you shall not be angry?" Joseph asked.

"I promise to *be* angry if you do not tell me," Rose replied.

Joseph sighed. "I have been training in all manners of fighting since I was eight with your captain of the guards, by order from your mother, the queen."

Rose gave the bandage a sudden, sharp tug.

"Ow! Careful, please! That is my sore arm!" Joseph cried.

"I am about to give you a sore nose in a minute!" Rose said rising to her feet. "You said you were told of this journey when you were thirteen, not eight!" Rose slapped Joseph on the shoulder, and he quickly withdrew in pain.

"I *was* told when I was thirteen!" he said. "I never knew what I was being trained for. I just knew that the queen wished it, and so I was."

Rose crossed her arms. "It never occurred to you to ask why?"

"Rose, I know we are close friends, but we do not have the same lives," Joseph said. "When the queen requests you do something, you do it. You do not ask why."

"You make my mother sound ghastly," Rose said with a hurt tone in her voice.

"No, Rose. It is just how it is," Joseph said. "We are the fortunate ones, who live under the rule of a kind and noble queen. But we are called 'subjects' for a reason. You have never known that life."

Rose stood silent. At once, she felt a distance between her and Joseph, wider than the one spanning the length of the troll's bridge. Without another word, Joseph slipped his shirt back over his arms and fastened the front. Rose walked over to the bridge and peered across, listening to the wind passing through the cavern.

"Brute, what is on the other side of this bridge?" Rose asked.

The troll turned toward her with a heavy sigh. "My home," he replied. "Or, at least, what was my home." Brute slumped back against a large rock and began to tell his story.

36

"My father and mother raised me in a cave in the mountainside beyond the bridge. My father built that bridge when it became apparent I was not to grow as large and hearty as he; he and Mother could simply leap across the cavern.

"It was eleven years ago…or was it twelve? Maybe twelve, since my mother died. After my father and I buried her, he hugged me for the first and last time and leaped into the skies. I never saw him come back down. I suspect he simply decided to go and be with Mother."

He paused to wipe his eyes.

"About three months ago, before the bad season began, I was in my cave, repairing a spearhead that had become chipped at the edge, when I heard a kind of 'trip-trap-trip-trap' on my bridge. I nearly fell over myself as I left my cave and went to see who it was. I had no idea what I was to say or do when I encountered whomever had come this far up the mountain, but what I did encounter, I was not expecting.

"In the middle of the bridge, stood a rather large and strong-looking mountain goat. By the size of it, I would have guessed it to be a full-grown adult, but it had the small horns of a baby. I walked out onto the bridge to shoo it back. As I approached, the goat seemed to notice the spear in my hand that, in my haste, I had carried with me from the cave and backed up a couple of steps. It let loose a long, loud bleat that echoed in the cavern, and that's when I heard more footsteps on the bridge.

"Another goat, much larger than the first, was walking to the center of the bridge, shaking it with each step. This goat was of an impossible size, yet by its horns, it could not have been any older than a young adult. It stopped just behind the smaller goat and stood there in what I can only describe as an air of agitation. I knew right then and there that both goats wanted something to fight. Maybe kill.

"Well, it was going to take more than two large goats to bully me from my bridge. When the second goat leaped over the first, I was ready and caught it by one of its horns. The first goat charged and rammed me in the knee, knocking me back a step or two. I began to jab at the goat with my spear as I held his bigger brother, but the little creature grabbed it in its mouth and broke it in half. I knew then that whatever had gotten in these goats' blood to make them so mad it was going to end up with one or all of us over the side if I did not put an end to it. I reached down with my free hand and grabbed the smaller one by the neck and hoisted it upward. Before I could decide what to do with the two kicking beasts, I heard a loud bellowing that could have woken the devil.

"On the other end of the bridge, stood the largest goat I have ever laid my eyes on. I dare say that this beast was as big as me. Its horns were thick and curved and it glared at me with its dark eyes. It did not wait to see what I was to do with the other two as it charged headlong onto the bridge. There was nowhere I could go but back. As I dropped his brothers on the bridge and turned to run back to the safety of the other side, I heard the animal leap and it soared over me and landed between my cave and I.

"For the first time in my life, I truly felt small and helpless. Had my father been there, he would have hurled all three of the monsters over the side without as much as a grunt. I did the best I could, but the truth is I was beaten. As I lay on the bridge, the three goats turned from me and stamped off into my cave. I knew then I had lost my home, and I crawled away. In the days since, I have lived unsheltered on this mountain. Every time I catch sight of them, they remain in an agitated mood. I have even seen them fight between each other or even with themselves, throwing their bodies against anything standing around them: a tree, a boulder, anything. Three nights ago, I awoke to hear them thrashing at each other from inside the cave. I have not seen or heard of them since.

"And now, here I sit."

After Brute finished his tale, he sat quietly. Rose looked toward the bridge.

"That is why you did not want us to cross," she said. "You wanted to protect us."

Brute looked at the young woman and gave a sad smile. "Yes, when I heard you approaching from further down the mountain, my first instinct was to observe you from a hidden place until I knew whether or not you were going to try and cross so I hung by the ropes under the bridge."

"That is quite a chance you took, my friend," Joseph said. "What if you had fallen?"

Brute laughed. "My father used to say something similar to that anytime he caught me doing it as a child, only he would be chasing me with a tree as he said it."

"Sounds like a rather gruff one, your father," said Snowflake.

"Oh, that he was," said Brute. "But he loved me, nonetheless."

While the others spoke, Rose remained looking at the bridge. The low clouds that had once concealed the cave on the other side were now gone, and she could see the black mouth looming in the distance. "Brute, is there another path beyond your cave?"

"No, miss," he said. "If you are looking for the route to the mountaintop just above and down the other side, I am afraid you passed it some time back."

"So, this is not our destination, then," Joseph said to the princess. "The skirt lies further up the mountain."

Rose nodded. She looked up at the rugged features of Brute's face. "You say you know not of why the goats have been so violent."

Brute shook his head.

"And you have not heard from them in three days' time?"

Brute nodded.

Rose got to her feet. "Snowflake, wait here with Wisher, please."

Joseph stood. "And where are we going?"

Rose walked over to Brute and held out her arm. "This charming gentleman is going to give a lady a grand tour of his home."

Chapter Five

It was many minutes of discussion, arguing, and pleading before Joseph and Brute gave in to Rose's wishes, and the trio crossed the bridge toward the mouth of the cave. Brute led Rose with Joseph close behind. Rose could feel the troll's chest heave in a sigh as they stepped off the bridge and onto the rocky outcropping in front of the dark hole in the mountainside.

The large muscles in Brute's arm hardened under Rose's grasp as the troll tensed himself. Rose looked up at Brute and smiled, patting his arm. Brute smiled back but did not relax. Rose realized from Brute's posture, he was not tensing for a fight. Rather, he was preparing to scoop her and Joseph up at a moment's notice and run back to the other end of the bridge.

"Brute," Rose said, "everything will be fine."

"You do not know that, little one," he replied. "But for you and your friends, I shall make sure it will be."

Now, it was Joseph who patted the troll, not in comfort, but in companionship. Brute responded with a curt nod, and the three stepped into the mouth of the cave.

Rose gasped as her eyes grew accustomed to the dark. The cave entrance had, indeed, been large enough for the easy passage of trolls, but the scale of the inside astounded her. Instead of a barren, rocky tunnel, a huge cavern surrounded her. A sharp strike echoed off the walls, and Rose spun around to see Brute lighting a large wall torch with a flint rock. He removed the torch from the wall and approached a small pit carved into the floor of the cave.

"Be ready, now," he said. "This will get their attention in a hurry."

Brute touched the torch to the pit, and with a swift *whoosh-ing* sound, flames sprang from the well, illuminating the entire main cavern. The interior had been crafted into a lavish home that reminded Rose of her own palace. Tapestries adorned the walls, and skillfully carved furniture filled the room. Carved into the far wall was a stove hearth with a chimney leading upward through the ceiling. In the walls around the main hall were whole rooms cut out of the mountain rock.

Rose heard a gasp from Brute. She followed his gaze, and for the first time, she noticed the destruction scattered in various parts of the cave. Smashed furniture littered the floor in places. Some tapestries hung by tatters. Brute slowly approached a painting smashed against the side of the main cavern and stood before it. Rose walked over and saw that it was a portrait of a powerful, yet feminine-looking troll holding a troll youngling.

"Your mother?" Rose asked.

"Yes," Brute replied so softly, Rose was unsure he answered at all. Quietly, he picked up the bent, torn painting and placed it gently on the stone table in the center of the room.

Slow, clacking hoofbeats sounded, and Rose and Joseph spun around in confusion. They echoed off the walls and seemed to come from everywhere. Brute, however, stood fast; his attention held to one dark room.

"There," he said pointing his torch. "The beasts are in there."

Inside the darkness, something seemed to stir. Rose and Joseph steeled themselves. Joseph spied a discarded blade lying on the floor nearby, and he quickly picked it up. It was a troll's dinner knife but Joseph held it as he would a short sword. Brute turned to look back at his companions one more time, then tossed the the torch into the dark room.

Rose, Joseph, and Brute motionlessly stared. As the light of the torch filled the room, they saw the pitiful sight of the three large goats; battered, beaten, and appeared to be half-dead. Only the largest stood. The other two lay on the floor of the room and only made the slightest movement to look at their observers.

Brute stepped between Rose and Joseph as a barrier between them and the large goat, his legs coiled and ready for any attack from the animal. He was concentrating on the goat so intently, he did not notice that Rose had stepped around him until Joseph called out.

"Rose, wait!"

Rose paid no attention to her friend. Silently, carefully, she approached the goat. It stood unmoving in the room, watching her. As she stepped closer, Rose could hear the air whistling out of its nostrils, and she could see its massive torso rise and fall in shuddering, heavy breaths. Rose could not figure out if the goat was angry, fearful, or in pain. Slowly, she held out her hand, knowing the goat could bite off her fingers before she could react.

The goat made no move as Rose's hand rested on the side of its nose. She could feel the beast shiver slightly under her touch. With her other hand, she reached around to brush the side of the goat's face. A sudden, sharp pain stung the palm of her hand, and she cried out, jerking her hand back. The goat jumped back, and quicker than she could have imagined, Brute and Joseph leaped to her side.

"Halt! All is well! It did not do anything," Rose said. Joseph and Brute stood still but ready.

Rose looked down at her hand. Jutting from the flesh of her palm was a large, thick thorn. She plucked it from her hand with a wince and dropped it to the ground.

Brute took her hand in his as he looked at the thorn on the cave floor. "Nasty devils," he grumbled. "Many thorn bushes grow up here. There is a great patch at the mountain top." Brute showed Joseph where he kept the oil and bandages, and soon, Brute wrapped Rose's puncture.

Rose stepped toward the opening of the room again. The large goat had now retreated to the side of its brothers. For a moment, it looked as if its legs would collapse from under it, but it steadied itself.

"Joseph, fetch me my hairbrush, would you?" Rose asked.

"Your...?" Joseph began.

Rose turned, an idea dancing in her eyes. "Hurry now, please."

"A moment," Brute offered. He disappeared into one of the dark rooms and soon re-emerged with a large brush, much like the brushes Joseph used on the stable of horses back at the palace. "Would this do?"

Rose's eyes lit up. "That would be perfect!" she said as she took the brush. She walked into the dark room.

The goat stood with quaking legs. Rose realized it was on the verge of falling over. "Easy, there," she whispered. "I am here to help you. You will let me help, will you not?"

The goat snorted once, as if in response. Rose stepped directly up to it and stood face to face with the large animal. Then Rose placed the brush in its thick, brown coat and ran the bristles through it.

Joseph and Brute watched as Rose walked around the goat, brushing as she went. Quite often, she would pull something from its fur or from the brush and place it on the ground. After a few minutes, the goat slowly sank to its knees and laid its head on the rocky floor.

"Brute, can you find some fresh water for them?" Rose asked. "They are near death."

"There is an inner well to a river that flows through the bottom of the mountain," he said. "It should not take me long." With that, Brute hurried further into the belly of the cave and disappeared down a passage.

Joseph approached Rose and the goat and knelt. "Rose, what is it? Why are they dying?"

In response, Rose pulled something from the goat's fur and placed it in Joseph's hand. It was another large thorn, like the one that had stuck Rose. She then pointed to a growing pile of thorns on the floor. "These poor animals have not eaten or drank in who knows how many days," she explained. "My guess is, they lived further up the mountain, perhaps at the very top. Some time ago, they must have encountered those bushes Brute mentioned earlier and gotten themselves tangled up in them. Their fur is laden with these wicked things. The pain was so great, they were in a constant state of rage and no longer sought any food or water; just something to stop the pain. In their agony, they attacked and drove our new friend from his home. And now, the poor dears are too weak to save themselves."

Brute returned with a large bucket half the size of Rose. As he approached, Rose felt the large goat stiffen and tremble beside her. "Shhhh, shhhh. He is a friend," she whispered to the animal. The trembling ceased. Rose motioned to Brute to kneel in front of the goat. As he did, he placed the bucket down in front of the goat's drooping head.

"Brute, you will have to raise his head to get it in the bucket," Rose said.

The troll hesitated for a moment, but then reached for the goat.

The goat bleated loudly, and it shook its horns at the troll's outstretched hands. Brute reached again and again the goat pulled back.

"It is no use," Brute grumbled. "The beast will not have anything to do with me."

The large goat snorted and swung its head to the side repeatedly. Rose, Joseph, and Brute exchanged worried glances. The goat seemed to be suffering from madness. Again, the goat shook his head over to the side. Rose followed the direction of the goat's motion, and her eyes fell upon the two other goats lying by the carved rock wall.

"His brothers!" Rose exclaimed. "He wants you to help his brothers first!"

Brute glanced over to the pitiful forms of the goats lying weakly on the floor. He reached over and gently scooped the smallest into his arms. Cradling the goat like a large child, Brute scooped handfuls of water from the bucket and poured it into its mouth. He did this for many minutes without any signs of life from the animal until it uttered a soft, weary sigh. The goat lifted its head and looked around. It gave a quiet but strong bleat to Brute.

Rose felt all the muscles in the large goat grow limp as it finally relaxed. Rose looked at Brute as the troll smiled down at the goat drinking from his hand. "I think you have three new friends, Brute," she said with a smile.

"No," Brute said as he returned her smile, "I have six."

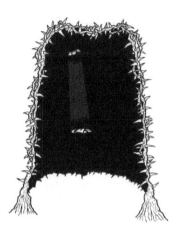

Chapter Six

A week had passed since Rose, Joseph, and Brute had entered the cave and found the dying goats. In that time, the three friends—now joined by Snowflake—had successfully nursed the animals back to health. The source of their rage and pain now gone, the three goats took on a more majestic quality. The largest was the elder brother of the other two and cared for them. The middle was the more curious of the three, and the youngest was the most rambunctious. As the days passed, the goats became more receiving of Brute's hospitality and even began to play games with the troll. Often, Brute would take his father's shield from the wall, and he and the three goats would have shoving contests. Rose, Joseph, and Snowflake often cheered for their large friend, and he would, on occasion, come out victorious, even against all three at once.

Finally, Rose knew she and her companions must continue their way up the mountainside. On a crisp, sunny morning Rose hugged Brute goodbye before making her way across the bridge.

"I am all the better to have met you, Brute," Rose said.

"And I you, little one," the troll said as he held back tears.

As Rose, Joseph, Snowflake, and Wisher crossed the bridge, the three goats bleated out their own farewell. Before losing sight of Brute's home as they travelled up the mountain, Rose turned and gave one final wave. Brute waved back as he patted the large goat standing next to him and for a moment—just one short moment—Rose thought she could see the faint sight of two larger trolls standing in the shadows of the cave entrance looking at her with gratitude in their eyes. Then, it was gone.

By mid-day, Wisher had grown weary from the thin mountain air robbing him of strength, and his steps grew more and more unsteady. Finding a wide spot along the trail, Rose and her companions stopped and sat on the ground. Snowflake walked up to Rose and rubbed against her hand.

"You look tired, Princess," he said.

"Yes, I am," the princess said. "But I have been tired before, and I shall be again."

Joseph offered Rose a drink from his pouch, which she took gratefully. She poured a slight amount in her hand for Snowflake and Joseph gave some to Wisher.

"Wisher is not going to make it much further up the mountain," he said. "The air is thinning, and the terrain is not getting any easier. A couple of times, I saw his hooves slide, and that would not do on some of the narrower parts of the trail."

Rose sat lost in thought. It was her assumption at the beginning of the quest that, whatever magic that created the map and gave Snowflake the gift of speech, would lead her to her goal; that it would help give her some sense that she was getting closer to the golden skirt. But she felt no such influence. Instead, she found herself as a thirteen-year-old woman, a great distance from her home and the family that loved her.

"Rose?' Joseph asked. "Is anything the matter?"

"What do you think they are doing right now?" Rose asked.

"Who?"

"Mother and Father," replied Rose. "Do you think they are well?'

Joseph sat next to his friend. "Indeed," he said. "Why should they not be? I will bet they had an uproarious Winter Festival, as usual. The king loves his festivals."

"As do I," Rose said. "Mother always took me to the top of the west tower during the festival to watch the people dancing below in the courtyard. The first time, as we stood up there, it began to snow, and the courtyard turned white in a matter of minutes. And yet, everyone kept dancing. It was such a pretty sight, like something out of a dream."

Joseph and Snowflake sat quietly, and Rose heaved a sigh. "I have not yet made it to the first part of my journey, and here I sit, a defeated little girl," she said. "A poor queen I will make."

"I have never seen you defeated, Princess," Joseph said, "and I am not seeing it now."

Rose turned and looked at the smiling face of her good friend. Then, out of the corner of her eye, Rose saw a shadow move in the distance. She looked past Joseph and stared up the trail. Catching her gaze, Joseph turned.

Standing firmly in the middle of the path was the large mountain goat. It gazed down at Rose and Joseph before deliberately turning and clopping up the trail.

"Joseph, stay here," Rose said, never taking her gaze off the goat, and stood.

"Rose, we do not know..."

"Joseph, I need you to stay here," Rose said. "We have nothing to tie Wisher to, and I do not want him wandering away."

Joseph opened his mouth to speak but closed it. Rose walked past him and started up the trail.

Rose followed the goat for the better part of a half-hour. As she walked, the growth of thorny bushes on the sides of the trail became more plentiful and dense. Every few minutes, Rose snagged an article of clothing on the sharp thorns and paused to unhook herself. Suddenly, Rose saw the goat stop at the top of a rise. She made her way swiftly and carefully to where the goat waited. She pulled herself over a small incline and stood next to the goat looking at a frightening sight in front of her.

At the top of the mountain, stretching on into the horizon, was a large, monstrous growth of thorny brush. Thorns as large as Rose's little finger and sharper than the sharpest dagger jutted from thick, twisted, black branches that wove together in angry knots. And at the front of the dark, gnarled mass that stood before Rose was an opening—an opening just large enough for a young woman.

For the first time in her journey, Rose shuddered with fear. The dark growth seemed to swell at her fear, and, for a moment, the branches seemed alive. Rose reassured herself that it was her emotions playing tricks on her, yet she could not bring herself to step forward.

The goat seemed to sense Rose's terror and gently placed its snout in her hand. Rose smiled and scratched his nose. "You know what awaits me in there, do you not?" she asked. Rose then kissed the animal on the forehead and walked into the dark brush.

The first thing Rose noticed when she entered the menacing growth was how little noise there was inside. Sounds she had been hearing in the background—wind, birds chirping, branches rustling—all faded away in the dense brush. Rose stood motionless as her eyes grew accustom to the dark. There was a path in front of her, though it didn't appear man-made. Rose carefully walked forward. She was twenty steps into the brush when the back of her hand caught on one of the thorns. She uttered a sharp cry as she pulled her hand away and felt warm blood trickling down her fingers. There was a rustling from behind her. Rose turned and what she saw caused her breath to catch in her throat.

The opening of the brush had closed itself. There was no way out.

For many moments, Rose did not move. Her mind felt numb to all emotions as she grasped the danger that she was now in. Gradually, fear crept through her body, and she wished for Joseph to be next to her to take her hand. The brave, bold woman inside her seemed to scamper away as if playing a cruel joke leaving behind a frightened, little girl who wanted someone to make the monsters go away.

Rose clutched at her breast and forced herself to relax her breathing. It took some time, but she calmed herself. The branches were not closing in. The thorns were not moving. Just fear playing its tricks again. She would be all right.

Rose started forward again into the heart of the dense growth. The path wound itself in a jumbled manner, and as Rose progressed, she found it growing narrower. The further she went, the more her clothes became entangled or torn in the grasping thorns. As she stepped around a tight bend, a thorn scratched her deeply, just above her left ear. Rose screamed in sudden pain and terror as she covered the gash with her hand. She heard more rustling and turned swiftly. The path behind her was now much smaller than it had been when she had walked through it.

A sob escaped Rose's lips as panic now set in. The branches moved. It was not her imagination. As much as she wanted to squeeze her eyes closed from the horrible sight, she stared wide-eyed in the darkness as the branches crept toward her. The thorns seemed to twist and grow longer as if in hunger for her blood.

Rose turned and ran. The path behind her was now closing violently, branches breaking from the force of their collapse and sending thorns shooting through the air like monstrous mosquitos. As Rose ran, more and more thorns tore at her clothes, hair, and skin. In her haste, Rose's foot caught on a root jutting from the ground. Screaming, she fell face down on the hard, rocky earth. Rose rolled over and saw the branches above her swarming down. The last bit of light faded as the growth closed in.

Rose laid her head back and shut her eyes. Tears rolled down as she waited for the end to take her. She thought of home, her friends, and her family. She thought of her father's hug and her sisters' laughter. She thought of Joseph, Snowflake, and Wisher waiting for her. She thought of her mother....

Rose, Precious.

Rose's eyes opened in the darkness as she thought of her mother's voice.

It is all right to be afraid, my girl.

Rose had heard those words before. She thought of the first time her mother took her to the tallest tower in the royal palace. Rose had only been five and with every step up the winding staircase, Rose had clung tighter to her mother's gown. When they had reached the top, she had seen a small, wooden stool standing next to the wall, overlooking the courtyard below. The queen walked over to the wall, but Rose stood by the doorway. Rose's mother came to her and led her to the stool. She stood in front of it looking down at her feet.

"Rose, Precious," she said, and Rose looked up with tears in her eyes. "It is all right to be afraid, my girl. Being afraid is part of being alive. But fear can stop us from experiencing life itself."

"Have you ever been afraid, Mother?"

"Oh, yes," she said. "I have been afraid many times. And I will be afraid again. But what I am never afraid of is *being* afraid. Many people live their entire lives being afraid and those people miss so much of what life can give them if they would only embrace that fear, place it aside and move forward."

The queen then turned from Rose and looked down to the courtyard below. Rose had looked at the stool for a moment or two before stepping onto it and pulling herself up to the top of the wall. When she looked down, she saw the entire courtyard alive with light, joy, dancing, and music. Then, at that very moment, the snow came. She held out her hands to the drifting white flakes and looked up at her mother's smiling face.

"You make me proud, Rose," her mother said. "You always have."

As the thirteen-year-old princess lay on the ground and the gnarled, tangled growth of the thorn brush completely enveloped her, she spoke.

"Thank you, Mother."

Rose suddenly sat upright, and the branches recoiled as if wilted by intense heat. She sprung to her feet, drew back a hand, and swiped at the cutting branches. Her hand and arm sliced through the dense growth, and the thorny branches exploded into particles of brown ash. The growth, sensing the strength in its former captive, tried to shrink away from Rose as she rampaged through it. She tore away branch after branch. Thorns broke and crumbled harmlessly in her hand. She ran through thick walls of needles as if they were not there. The light became brighter and brighter as the brush shrank and withered away.

And then, it was gone.

Rose stood on the mountaintop. Her shining eyes looked outward from a grime-streaked face. A smile crossed her lips as she thought of her home in the unseen distance. And in her heart, Rose knew her mother would be on the tallest tower looking back toward her.

Rose looked down at her hands now covered in brown ash and blood from her many cuts. But something else caught her attention. Though the sun was in front of her, her body cast its shadow forward as if there was another source of light from behind. Rose turned around and shielded her eyes from an dazzling glare.

There, on a stone alter that had once been standing in the heart of the dark brush, hung the golden skirt. The light of the sun gleamed off it in a bright glow.

As if in a dream, Rose walked toward the altar. She reached out with her soiled hands and picked up the heavy skirt. It was solid, spun gold, but it was also more. In its fibers, Rose could feel warmth that reminded her of the summer sun coming from it. She closed her eyes and released a long, satisfied sigh.

Chapter Seven

As the spring season surrendered to summer, Rose found herself celebrating her fourteenth birthday with little fanfare. After the journey back down the mountain and through the kingdom of Merc, Rose and her companions were too weary to consider any sort of celebration, large or small. Joseph did manage to surprise Rose with a piece of sweet bread he traded for at the last house they had stopped at before leaving the kingdom. Rose insisted on sharing the small slice with Joseph and Snowflake, and the trio sat by the side of the road as they ate quietly.

"How long will we do this, Rose?" Joseph asked.

"Do what?" Rose responded.

"Wander without direction or purpose," he said. "The map is useless now. Snowflake knows not of what lies ahead or where to even go."

The cat mumbled under his breath as he slowly nibbled on the bread.

Rose swallowed her last morsel and sat in thought. She had been troubled when she and Joseph could find no indication of where they were to go at the top of the mountain where she had retrieved her first prize. It was torturous debating on whether to wait at the mountaintop for a sign or to journey back down to the land below, but eventually, the trio began back the way they came. Even a brief stay at Brute's cave to heal and rest did not give Rose any reason to believe leaving the mountain was not the right choice. But now that they were outside the kingdom at the mountain's feet, she found doubt creeping into her mind.

"I wish I had an answer to give you, Joseph," Rose finally said.

"Hallo there!" a cracked voice called from the road. Rose, Joseph, and Snowflake turned to see the bent form of an old woman walking in their direction. The woman's face was filled with lines and wrinkles with two soft, hazel eyes peering from under the folds of her skin. Her mouth stretched into a wide grin that revealed three lonely but beautifully polished teeth. On her back was a large sack, and she held onto it with two, white-knuckled hands.

"Hallo!" she called again. "I say, you do not see many people this far outside of Merc even in early summer. Still too cold for long walks!"

Rose and Joseph got to their feet and approached the woman. "I must agree with you, my lady," Rose said. "You look rather chilled yourself."

"Eh! No worries, no worries," the old woman said as she continued her shuffling pace. Despite the joyous tone of the woman's voice, Rose could see the weariness on her face.

"Will you sit a moment?" Rose asked. "You look like you could use some rest and company."

"Well, are you not a dear?" the woman said smiling. "But I have important people to meet with up the road a piece. I am afraid they cannot wait."

Rose looked to Wisher and uttered a sharp whistle. The horse immediately was at her side. "Then let us carry you," she said.

"Oh, that is very gracious of you, dear, but I will be no burden on anybody," the old woman said.

Joseph gently took the woman's hand in his. "The burden appears to be on you," he said. Without another word, he lifted the sack from her and hefted it onto Wisher's back.

"My, my, that is a fine, strong horse you have there, my lad," the woman said as she looked at Wisher. "He will fetch a bag of silver at the traders, I would bet."

"His name is Wisher," Rose said, "and he is my steed."

The old woman turned to Rose with regard. "Is he, now?" she asked. "You must be a woman of fine standing to have such a horse."

Rose saw a brief flash of worry on Joseph's face. "Yes, I suppose I am," Rose said.

"Eh! Say no more, dear," the woman said. "I am no snooper."

After much discussion and prodding, Joseph and Rose helped the old woman onto Wisher. They both carried their supply packs as Rose led Wisher on the road and Joseph carried Snowflake on his shoulder.

After some time, the woman called out, "My dear, here is where I need to be!" She pointed with one long finger to a bare spot by the side of the road.

Rose led Wisher to the spot, and she and Joseph helped the old woman down. She thanked them for their kindness as she sat on the cold earth.

"You do not meet many people of your age anymore who are as gracious as you have been," she said. "Too much reading, I say."

The long, spidery fingers of the woman began to fumble and fidget at the drawstring of her side pouch. Without a word, Joseph gently touched her hands, stilling them. The old woman smiled as Joseph undid her pouch for her.

"I apologize for my manners, but now that I am seated, I feel a little light in the head," the woman said as she pulled from her pouch a dried, crusty slice of rye. "All I need is a nibble and I will be strong again."

Now, it was Rose who held the woman's hands. "Joseph, see what I have in my supply pack, please."

Joseph was on his feet before the woman could protest. "Oh, now, you need not trouble yourselves, please."

"No trouble, my lady," Rose said. Joseph brought Rose's pack, and Rose produced the last of a wrapped cheese and some soft bread. Joseph, in turn, found a single remaining apple and salted ham.

As the woman protested, Rose and Joseph prepared a lunch for her from the remaining supplies. Even with the measly morsels, Rose was quite proud of the plate they were able to prepare.

The old woman's eye lit up with delight. She regarded her stale slice of bread with new disgust and tossed it to Snowflake. "Here you are, pussikins," she said. "Enjoy."

Snowflake glared at the woman and the bread with annoyance and sulked off into the bushes.

"What a nice kitty," the woman said as she ate.

After the woman finished her lunch, she slowly got to her feet with some assistance from Rose and Joseph. "Well, now," she said as she stretched, "I guess it is time I went on my way and you on yours."

"Ah, but my lady," Rose said, "what of the important people you are to meet here?"

The woman smiled warmly, and she suddenly seemed more youthful and stronger than a moment before. "Have you not guessed yet, Princess? I was supposed to meet you."

Rose and Joseph stood in silence as the woman chuckled to herself and reached inside of her side pouch and took something out. She placed an unseen object in Rose's hands and gently curled the princess' fingers around it.

"Go where you find the brothers and sisters of what I have given you," she said. "There, you will find the next object of your quest."

The old woman turned from Rose and Joseph and walked back up to the road.

"Wait!" called Joseph. "You forgot your sack!"

Without turning around, the woman called back, "It belongs to you now, young master. Use it well," and walked away.

Rose and Joseph stood looking out at the road. Slowly, Rose opened her hands and looked down at what she held.

"What is that?" Joseph asked as he stared at the strange but beautiful object. "A painted rock?"

"It is a seashell," Rose whispered. "Father brought me one like this from one of his voyages with King Tobias." Rose looked at Joseph with a sparkle in her eye that a small child would have on the eve of a birthday.

"We are going to the sea, Joseph."

Chapter Eight

In all her dreams, Rose had never imagined a sight such as what lay before her. Rolling green hills and massive forests covered her native land so the flat, vast gulf of blue water that stretched into the horizon held her motionless in awe. Crashing waves on the beach roared pleasantly in her ears. The sand under and over her feet played with her sensations. The air smelled of saltwater as the warm breeze caressed her face. Rose knew it was well into the heart of winter in her homeland, but here, snow and cold were mere memories and daydreams.

"So beautiful," Rose whispered. She held out her arms as the wind picked up, and the waves crashed on the shore. Snowflake quickly retreated behind Rose as the water rushed up. Joseph, sitting in the sand, giggled like a child as the sea spray struck the cat's face.

"So *wet*," the cat grumbled before hurrying away from the next wave washing toward them.

"When I am queen, my first act will be to bring our people to this place," Rose said.

Joseph grinned. "That is the first time since we began this adventure that you have spoken of your impending rule, Rose."

Rose looked at Joseph with a smile. She walked over and sat in the sand next to him. She ran her fingers through the soft surface of the shore, picked up a moist clump, and let it fall back through her fingers. "I did not really think about it until just now. I was standing there looking out at the beautiful blue water, and I just thought how shameful it was that everyone in Ametheria couldn't see this, and that, as Queen, I could rectify that. Do you think I will make a good queen, Joseph? The truth, please."

"You will make an fine queen, Princess; one I would be proud to serve under," Joseph replied. He then rose to his feet. "My stomach is about to get the better of me. Care for lunch?"

Joseph walked back to the grassy rise at the edge of the shore where Wisher waited. Snowflake padded close behind. "What shall it be today, Rose?" Joseph asked as he removed the sack the old woman left with them months ago from Wisher's back. "Lady's choice."

"Here, now. When do I get to use this enchanted sack?" said Snowflake.

"When we are sure you will choose something other than raw fish," Joseph replied.

Rose turned and reclined on her elbows in the sand. "Why not roast duck in a sweet glaze, fresh boiled greens, and buttered rolls? With red wine, of course."

64

"Roast duck?" Joseph asked in mock horror. "We are by the ocean. Surly you mean lobster?"

"For dinner, perhaps. This is lunch. And you did say lady's choice."

"Have you even had wine, dear Rose? It might be too much for one as young as yourself—" Joseph's words were cut short as a clump of sand struck him on the shoulder. Rose laughed as Joseph hid behind Wisher for protection. "Your mistress is a sour, old hag at such a young age," he told the horse and Wisher snorted in annoyance. He carried the sack over to the edge of the sand as Rose walked over and seated herself on the grass. Joseph opened the sack and reached in. He hissed sharply.

"Are you all right?" Rose asked.

"Yes, yes," Joseph said as he pulled from the sack a magnificent silver platter. On the platter was a freshly golden-roasted duck glistening in a sugar glaze surrounded by steaming green beans and piping-hot dinner rolls dripping with butter as if all had just been prepared in the palace kitchens. "The platter was a bit hot, is all."

He sat the platter between him and Rose. As she began to pull apart the duck and shred some of the tender meat for Snowflake, Joseph pulled from the sack two goblets and a bottle of red wine.

"Wine, as requested," Joseph said with a haughty flourish. Rose giggled as Joseph struggled with the cork, finally pulling it from the bottle with a sighing pop. Snowflake nibbled on duck meat as Joseph poured the red liquid into the goblets. "Wonderful business, this sack. Any meal upon request. How many more enchanted items do you think we shall be granted on this journey?"

"I doubt none as useful as this," Rose said. She brought the goblet to her face and sniffed the red drink inside. For a moment—just one moment—she could see the banquet table of her home, her sisters seated around her in the warm candlelight laughing and talking of small yet important things, while her parents sat at each end of the table watching and smiling. Rose always knew they watched them enjoying their time together but never wondered until now if they were aware of her knowing. She put the goblet to her lips and drank.

"So, what do you think?" Joseph asked.

"Tastes like home," she replied.

After lunch, Rose and Joseph brought Wisher down to the shore, and Rose spent the afternoon riding up and down the coastline as Joseph and Snowflake sat and watched.

"How will we know what to look for?" Joseph called out as Rose began to ride past. Rose pulled the reigns and patted Wisher as she dismounted.

"These trials seem to find us as much as we find them," she said. "I say we make camp here. If nothing makes itself known to us by tomorrow, we move further down the shoreline."

Joseph shrugged and lay back on the sand. "I can think of far worse courses of action to take. But if you insist."

Rose playfully kicked sand on her friend, and in moments, they began to chase and toss sand at each other, both laughing wildly as they did so. Amid their play, Rose stopped as she spied something further down the beach.

Joseph, moments from dousing his friend over the head with two handfuls of sand, paused. "What is it?"

"That was not there before," Rose said more to herself as she walked toward the water. Joseph let the sand slip from his hands and followed the princess. After a moment, Joseph spied what drew Rose's attention.

A dark shape lay close to the water, half buried in the sand. They approached the object cautiously at first. The sunlight reflecting from the white sand made it difficult to clearly see what it was. As they closed the gap between the object and themselves, they realized they were looking at the protruding head of a large, half-buried fish. Its mouth opened and closed as its glassy eyes seemed to peer into the distance.

"Do you think this one talks?" Joseph asked.

Rose did not reply. She kept staring at the fish as it gasped slower and slower. She dropped to her knees next to the fish and began to scoop away the sand that held it fast. Joseph hopped over to the fish's other side and did the same. It took many minutes to uncover the enormous creature, and its gaping mouth now barely moved.

"Hurry. The water," Rose said.

Joseph nodded, and together, the two lifted the fish from the sandy hole and carried it toward the crashing waves. They waded in until the water came to their waists.

"This should be far enough," Rose said and they released the fish into the salty water. Immediately, the fish jumped to life and flicked its tail, shooting it through the water and spraying Rose and Joseph.

"That is a lot of thanks, for you!" Joseph said as he spat ocean water from his lips.

Rose looked out at the water around her in anticipation. She could see no sign of the fish.

"Come, Rose," Joseph said. "Let's go back and dry out our..."

Suddenly, the ocean surface burst in front of Rose and Joseph, completely drenching them. After they wiped the water from their eyes, they saw in front of them the shape of a large, bare-chested man standing waist deep in the water. The man smiled down at the two soggy persons in front of him.

"Friends!" the man cried. "You have done me a grand service. For that, I shall forever be grateful. Be privileged to have won the favor of King Tangaroa!"

Rose and Joseph, silent, stared at the naked man before them. King Tangaroa stood motionless, still smiling. As the silence continued, the king's brow furrowed.

"King Tangaroa!" he repeated. Again, only the sound of the waves rushing the shore responded. "Master of the Seas! Lord of the Oceans! Wrestler of Whales! Friend to Shellfish, maybe?"

Joseph was the first to find his voice. "Your...Highness, may I inquire as to the nature of your being here and, if you will forgive me, whether or not you are wearing any bathing garments in front of the lady, here?"

King Tangaroa paused a moment before laughing heartily. "A couple of potatoes you are!"

Rose and Joseph looked at each other in confusion.

"Potatoes?" Rose asked.

"Never seen the majesty of the Great Maker's oceans before," the king declared. "For if you had..." Faster than Rose and Joseph could see, the king disappeared under the water. Just as quickly, he sprang from the surface a full ten feet into the air, the long, silvery tail extending from his waist flapping in the sun.

"...you would have heard of me!" he said as he dove back into the water with a splash that once again soaked Rose and

Joseph, too stunned to wipe the water from their faces. The mer-king popped back to the surface like a cork, laughing at Rose and Joseph's expressions. "You two truly do not get around much, do you?"

"Until recently, no," Rose said before curtseying the best she could in waist-deep waters. "My apologies if I or my companion offended you, Your Highness."

"Offended me?" the king replied. "The fair maiden who saved my life from that blasted witch's curse? Nay!"

"Witch's curse?" asked Joseph.

"Aye, my lad," said Tangaroa, "a foul beast indeed she was. My best warriors fell before her putrid, evil horde until I led the charge and slayed the wicked wretch. With her last breath, she cast a spell of transformation over me, and I have wandered aimlessly across my kingdom, seeking a pure soul to break the spell. By mere happenstance, I became swept along the shore currents and mired in the sand just before you spotted me. Another minute, and I would have surely perished!"

"I am glad to have been in your service, Your Highness," said Rose.

"As am I!" King Tangaroa said with a broad grin. "And now, I must take my leave of you, for I have been away from my palace for too long, and I am anxious to see my lovely daughters again. Farewell, my friends!"

King Tangaroa turned and held his arms out to dive into the sea, when Rose called out, "A moment, King Tangaroa!"

"Yes, little one?"

"I do not think it purely luck that we came across you in your moment of need. I am on a quest to find my coronation gown, for I am Princess Rose of Ametheria, and I am on my journey to become queen. I think perhaps you may help me."

King Tangaroa stroked his beard in thought. "You do, eh? I know of Ametheria, and you have come far for a mere gown, Princess."

"Not just any gown, dear King. The pieces of the gown were spun of pure gold."

The mer-king's eyebrows suddenly raised upward. "By the ocean's blue heart! You are referring to the golden shirt!"

Joseph and Rose exchanged an excited look. "Yes, Your Highness, a shirt is one of the pieces I seek."

"It is fate, then!" the king declared. "Many years ago, while exploring a sunken vessel, my daughters discovered such a garment. Its fabric was so brilliant, it shined even in the darkest depths of my kingdom."

Suddenly, King Tangaroa disappeared under the surface. He reappeared down the shoreline where some sea foam had gathered. Joseph and Rose watched in amazement as the mer-king sculpted the foam into a large, round bubble. When he finished, he carried the bubble over to Rose and Joseph.

"Please," the king said, gesturing to the bubble, "and I shall show you both the wonders of my kingdom under the water's surface."

Rose paused. "You mean to take us with you in this?"

"Why, yes!"

Rose looked at the seemingly fragile structure. She placed a hand against it and was surprised by its flexibility and sturdiness. She pushed harder and saw her hand pass though the surface as the bubble stayed intact. Joseph felt of the bubble, as well, and laughed.

"Incredible substance," he said. He then looked at Rose. "I guess it would do me no good..."

Rose smiled and shook her head.

"Luck be with you, then," he said and kissed her on the forehead. He then turned and started back to the shore. King Tangaroa watched him leave with a frown.

"Is the young lad afraid? I can assure you...."

"No assurances needed," Rose said. "These parts of my quest must be accomplished by myself alone."

"A brave lass. I think my daughters will like you," the king said with a smile.

Rose pushed thought the membrane of the bubble and climbed inside. King Tangaroa motioned for Rose to sit back, and he pulled the bubble along as he swam out and down into the sea, both he and Rose sinking below the water's surface.

Chapter Nine

The reunion of King Tangaroa and his family was one of the most precious moments Rose had ever witnessed. The mermaid princesses, all seven of them, refused to stop hugging their father for nearly an hour. A celebration began in the undersea kingdom with Rose finding herself the guest of honor. Due to her inability to leave the safety of her bubble, two guards served as her escorts and carried her around the kingdom, often bringing replacement bubbles to refresh her air supply.

Though the depths of the water blocked out the sun, the kingdom glowed with a luminescent stone that covered most of the underwater buildings. Heat vents in the ocean floor warmed the seawater in the kingdom like the baths Rose enjoyed back in Ametheria. The beauty and brilliance of the undersea city was astounding, and, for a time, Rose found herself forgetting her quest.

"Your kingdom is a wonder of the eyes and a feast of the mind, Your Highness," Rose said to the undersea king.

"Very kind of you to say," replied King Tangaroa. "I imagine the sights you have seen on your journey would be as wondrous to myself and my people, as well."

"Perhaps," Rose replied, her voice trailing off as the remembrance of why she was there re-entered her mind. "And, as much as I despise bringing an end to this marvelous experience…"

"Ah, of course!" the king said. Gathering his daughters together, the king brought them and Rose to a chamber in his palace. The king relieved the two escorts and asked them to wait outside the chamber.

"My dears," the king said to his children, "this heroic young lady, whom you have to thank for returning your father to you, is on a grand, magical quest!"

The seven princesses shivered with delight. It had been a long while since they had last heard a tale told by their father, and he had a most exciting way of spinning a story.

"She, like yourselves, is a princess…"

The princesses gasped and chuckled in surprise.

"…and her quest has brought her here, to our grand kingdom, to obtain a piece of her coronation gown: a gown spun from gold."

The eyes of all seven mermaids lit with understanding.

"The golden shirt!" said one.

"From the wreckage!" uttered another.

"The one I found!" said yet another.

"You mean *I* found!" said the eldest daughter.

73

"Did not!" accused the youngest.

"You are always claiming others' deeds, Argyra!" said another.

"Daughters!" King Tangaroa bellowed in such a voice, waves crashed on the ocean surface above. "What a shameful display!"

"It is quite all right, Your Highness," Rose said. "It reminds me of the arguments between my sisters and me."

"You have sisters, too?" asked one mermaid princess.

"How many?" asked another.

"I am the eldest of five."

The oldest mermaid princess, Argyra, smirked. "Difficult being the firstborn, is it not? Having to be the most responsible, the most proper, the most intelligent...,"

"The most snobbish," one of the sisters chimed in.

Argyra glared at her giggling siblings, looking for the one who dared to humiliate her. Rose did her best to hide her own smirk.

"Yes, indeed. This journey is a responsibility I have being the eldest. I have to use my wits to uncover the clues for me to continue onward."

"Is that why you saved Father?" one princess asked.

"No. When I saved your father, I did not know who he was or of the golden garment that waited here. All I knew was that a creature was in distress, and I did what I felt was right."

"So, then, it is more luck than your 'wits' that led you down here?" Argyra said in a mildly challenging tone.

For a moment, Rose felt her cheeks flush—a reaction her sister Blossom could always manage to get from her—and she took a slight breath before speaking. "You might look at it that way. Another is that compassion led me here."

"Luck. Blind luck," Argyra dismissed.

Now Rose could not hold back the redness in her face. "As I said, one could look at it in that manner."

"I do."

"Daughter," King Tangaroa said in a low voice that could freeze the water surrounding them, "I suggest you cease insulting my savior and retrieve what she came here for."

"Of course," the princess said as she turned away, "I just did not want her to feel she had not earned it, was all."

Before Rose could stop herself, she said, "And how would I earn it?"

In a flash, Argyra spun around and was at the bubble looking in with sharp eyes. "A battle of wits. You are supposed to use your wits, are you not?"

Had Rose not felt so frustrated with the princess, she would have noticed the king's anger boiling at his rude daughter. "What do you suggest?" she asked.

"A storytelling contest."

Suddenly, the chamber was alive with excitement from the other princesses as they whispered to each other in eager tones.

"What are the rules?"

"Each of us has to tell a story based on suggestions by my sisters. The best storyteller wins the shirt."

Suddenly, one of the king's large hands gripped the firstborn princess by the shoulder. "Do not reply, Princess Rose of Ametheria," he said before turning to his daughter. "You and I are to have words. Now."

The king spun the princess around and began to lead her from the chamber. Before they could exit, Argyra turned her head and gave Rose an arrogant smile. It was the exact smile

Blossom always gave Rose whenever she successfully enraged her with a hurtful insult.

"I accept," Rose said.

The king stopped short and turned, placing one hand on his head and shaking it, which pulled Rose completely out of her rage. The realization of what she had done began to sink in as Argyra crossed her arms.

"Lovely," the oldest princess said. "I will inform our royal servants to spread the news." With that, she swam past Rose and out into the open waters of the kingdom.

The other mermaid princesses hurried from the chamber, asking one another what they were wearing to the contest. In moments, only Rose and King Tangaroa remained.

"I...apologize for my daughter," the king said. "I indulge her too much. She is intelligent, that one, but she has no manners."

"It is I who should apologize, Your Highness. I did not conduct myself as a princess or a guest and let my anger control my tongue, much to my regret."

"The regret may last longer than you think. Dismissing a challenge is impossible, even by me. Argyra is the cleverest storyteller in our kingdom. She has never lost a contest, and I fear that is where her...*superiority* springs from."

Rose's eyes fell downward. All at once, the kingdom didn't seem so bright and wondrous. It seemed dark and confining. After a moment, she looked up at the king.

"Well," she said, "maybe it is time to teach her a little humility."

Jousting was never one of Princess Rose's favorite contests to watch. She considered it less a contest of skill and more a violent, loud spectacle made more so by the cheering crowds that gathered to watch. It was then surprising to Rose when the same cheering seemed to thunder through the undersea kingdom as she and Princess Argyra were brought out into a bowl-shaped arena. Mer-people surrounded them, all eager for the contest to begin. Several mer-men shouted encouragement to Argyra as she arrived with Rose in the center of the arena. She waved to her fans and smiled pleasantly, surprising Rose who didn't think her capable of making anything other than a sneer or a smirk. Soon, the king and the other mermaid princesses arrived and gathered themselves on a platform on one end of the arena. A raise of his hand hushed the crowd.

"May this contest of stories bring forth thought and imagination to our kingdom and its inhabitants. My subjects, I give you our champion: Princess Argyra!"

Through the wall of the bubble, Rose could feel the vibrations of the shouting and cheering from the spectators. She could see the energizing effect it was having on her competition and she began to feel more than a little nervous.

"And her competitor, the first land-dweller to ever visit the depths of these waters: Princess Rose of Ametheria!"

Rose could make out some polite cheering, mostly coming from the princesses, but an occasional shout of "potato" was impossible to miss. Rose glanced over at Princess Argyra and saw her glaring back at her. Rose looked away and concentrated on the king as he spoke.

"One by one, each of my daughters will give the storyteller a subject that must be used in her story. Once a storyteller begins, they cannot stop until they reach the conclusion. Any rest or pause in the telling will disqualify the contender. After both stories are told, it will be up to you, my loyal subjects to choose the winner."

Upon hearing the words "my loyal subjects," Rose's nervousness soared. It had not occurred to her until that moment that Princess Argyra may be deemed champion, simply due to the unwillingness of the crowd to pick anyone other than the daughter of their king, but before Rose could quiet the doubts in her mind, the king continued.

"Our champion will now receive her story subjects and commence with regaling us with her intellect and cleverness!"

Rose barely heard the story suggestions given to Argyra by her sisters. Her own breathing seemed to be resounding louder and louder in her surrounding bubble. Her heart seemed to be pounding from her chest as she watched Argyra spin her tale, dramatically gesturing at the heights of her story. Rose thought she could make out something about a...*sharp*? Shark? It was attacking a sliver...no, *silver* goddess. Rose couldn't make sense of it. She couldn't think. She watched as Argyra seemed to drift in and out of focus. The undersea world seemed to spin. The air felt heavy....

Rose's eyes widened.

My air is gone.

The crowd cheered at the conclusion of Argyra's story. Everything grew dark as Rose pitched forward.

Suddenly, a hand grasped Rose by the arm, and she felt herself pulled through one bubble and into another. The sudden rush of fresh air in her lungs snapped Rose's eyes open, and she filled her lungs with a loud gasp. A coughing spell followed as she looked toward the guard who had pulled her to safety.

"My apologies, Princess. I did not mean to tarry so," he said with an air of indifference. Rose simply nodded at him as he turned to swim away, and, for an instant, she saw a look pass between the guard and Argyra: a look of sly satisfaction. With that, all Rose's nervousness suddenly vanished and determination rose within her.

"Princess Rose?" the king asked in a worried voice. "Are you well? Should we cease?"

Rose straightened, and, for the first time, saw Argyra shrink ever so slightly away from her presence.

"I am ready for your daughters' delightful and witty suggestions," she said in a strong, pleasant voice.

The king gestured to his daughters as they began to shout out:

"Your story must contain a brave knight."

"And a battle!" said another princess.

"People in peril!" said another.

"It must have a moral," said another.

"Stories with morals are depressing!"

"I like morality stories."

"You would."

"A dragon!" said the second youngest princess.

"There are no such things as dragons!"

"Well in this story there is!"

Rose counted each suggestion as she locked them away in her mind. She looked up at the royal court, and her gaze fell upon the youngest princess, who looked to be no more than three years of age. "Your Grace, what is your suggestion?"

In a low voice, the little princess said, "My name."

"What is your name?"

"Nixie."

Rose smiled. "That is the most beautiful name I have ever heard, Nixie." The princess looked up and grinned. Rose silently went over each suggestion. Finally, she spoke.

"Once upon a time, there lived a dragon in a mountain-side cave. The dragon was a gigantic beast with fiery-red scales; a truly ferocious-looking creature.

"Located next to the mountain was a village. Terror of the dragon filled the hearts of the villagers. Each day they would see the monster fly to and from its cave as it went out for food.

"'It will burn our village!'

"'It will eat our livestock in a single day!'

"'It will sweep us all away with one swipe of its tail!'

"The people would shout and scream these same words day after day every time the dragon's shadow fell across the village. And day after day, the dragon never burned a house and ate no livestock. The dragon always fed on the wild animals of the nearby forest and didn't give the village one thought or look as it flew overhead.

"Then, one day, a brave knight from the nearby kingdom rode into town on a great, white steed. The knight's armor was of the shiniest steel, his shield the strongest iron, and his sword the sharpest blade.

"The villagers all gathered around the knight as he dismounted. 'Word has reached my ears that you have a dragon problem,' said the knight. 'I am here to slay this monstrous beast for you.'

"A cheer went up from the crowd. The villagers patted the knight on the back and shook his hand as they told him the location of the dragon's lair. Amongst the cheering villagers stood a young girl. She was not cheering but looked thoughtful. The knight took notice of the silent girl and approached her.

"'Young lady,' said the knight, 'are you not pleased that I am to bravely vanquish your dragon for you?'

"The little girl, named Nixie, looked back up at the knight. 'But, Sir Knight, the dragon has not done anything to us.'

"The villagers grew quiet. They looked away from the little girl, ashamed and embarrassed at her words. The knight, however, chuckled with a knowing smile. 'It has not done anything *yet.*'

"The villagers began to shout again; not in joy this time, but fear.

"'It could burn our village!'

"'It could eat all our livestock in a single day!'

"'It could sweep us all away with one swipe of its tail!'

"The little girl lowered her eyes as the knight patted her head. 'You will see, little one,' he said. 'There is nothing worse than having a dragon around. No good ever comes from them.' With those words the knight mounted his horse, waved goodbye to the cheering villagers and rode toward the mountain.

"Many days later, in the cave on the mountaintop, the red dragon slept peacefully. It dreamed of clear skies to fly in and its family back in the homeland. It did not hear the approaching footsteps of the knight as he crept closer to the dragon. Carefully, the knight drew his sword, ready to slay the creature before him.

"Suddenly, the dragon opened one yellow eye, then the other. It saw the knight three steps away holding his sword. The dragon raised his head before the knight could strike. The knight poised his shield ready for the fiery blast that he knew was sure to come. But, to the knight's surprise, the dragon spoke instead.

"'Hello, there,' said the dragon. 'I did not hear you come in. Is there something I may do for you, Sir Knight?'

"'Yes, foul beast, you may feel the edge of my sword as I slay you!' shouted the knight.

"The dragon looked at him with regard. 'Slay me? What have I done to deserve death?'

"'You are a dragon, and, therefore, a blight on our land! Prepare for battle!'

"The dragon again regarded the knight and his words. 'I have committed no crime, and I am offended at your opinion of me. Please leave as you came, Sir Knight.'

"The knight's mouth hung open in shock. No dragon had ever spoken to him in this manner. He had slain many before they even had a chance to utter a sound. 'Dragon! I am a knight of His Majesty's royal court, and I shall slay you!'

"The dragon sat fully upright. With a sigh, it said, 'Very well. If you must fight, then I shall oblige you for no dragon rolls over to die for anyone.'

"And so, the knight and the dragon did battle in the cave on the mountaintop. The fight was so fierce everyone in the village below could hear it. The fight raged for over three days and nights. Then, all was quiet. For many days, the villagers mourned what surely had been the death of the heroic knight until, one morning, the knight rode into the village, his face slack with weariness but his eyes sparkling with triumph.

"'Your dragon menace is no more,' the knight said. 'I have done a knight's duty, and I shall take my leave confident that your days of fear and turmoil are behind you.' And with that, the knight rode away with the cheers of the villagers behind him.

"And there would normally be the end of our story. But alas, for the poor people of the village, it is not. You see, dragons are territorial creatures. While the red dragon lived in the land of the village, no other dragons came near. But, nary ten days from the death of the red dragon, a green dragon came to live in the cave at the mountaintop. This creature was not as peaceful as the red dragon and as soon as it discovered the village below...

"...it burned the houses...

"...ate all the livestock in a single day...

"...and swept everyone away with a swipe of its tail.

"And the moral of our story is," Princess Rose said as she turned and gave her storytelling rival a meaningful smile, "let sleeping dragons lie."

And, for one long moment, all was quiet. Then, the cheering started. Princess Argyra looked around in stunned silence as the cheering became louder and louder, cascading down on the two princesses in a swelling of noise unlike any ever heard in the arena before.

"The winner!" King Tangaroa called, his arm raised toward the princess in the bubble. His daughters swam down to Rose and surrounded her with congratulations and praise. It did not escape Rose's attention that the sisters took exceptional glee in making sure their older sister heard every word. And Rose, as ashamed as she felt of this, could not help but share a little of that glee.

A hush fell over the arena then, and the princesses parted ways as two royal guards entered carrying a bundle wrapped in a blanket of seaweed. They brought the bundle before the king, who carried it to Rose. Gently, he pushed the bundle through the bubble and into Rose's hands. The mermaids gathered around as Rose delicately removed the wrapping.

Even in the depths of the sea, the golden shirt shone brilliantly. Even Argyra, her face sullen with defeat, could not help but look with wide eyes. Rose looked upward at King Tangaroa's smiling face. "Thank you," she said.

"Where shall your quest take you now?" King Tangaroa asked.

"I do not yet know. I suspect that knowledge shall come when I least expect it."

"Maybe the markings on the back will tell you," the second youngest princess said.

All eyes turned toward her.

"Markings?" Argyra asked. "What markings?"

"On the back of the garment." The second youngest looked at her sisters. "Surely you have noticed them? They appeared before when the sun's rays cut through the water and shone upon it."

Rose held the shirt close to the surface of the bubble and she and the mermaids quickly examined the back of the shirt for any markings or lettering but could find nothing in the swirling patterns of gold.

"You say you saw them when the sun lit upon it?" Rose asked.

"Why, yes. Once I took the shirt from the holding room and swam it close to the surface to look at it. When I looked at the back, I noticed certain parts of the gold fabric shone in a manner the others did not. It looked like some curious form of drawing."

Rose touched the back of the garment and closed her eyes. As she felt around, she thought she could detect a pattern of texture different from the rest of the gold weaving.

"Again, you have my thanks," Rose said. She looked up at King Tangaroa. "It seems it is my time to take my leave of you and your wonderful family, Your Highness."

Rose said her goodbyes to the princesses, and she and King Tangaroa left the kingdom under the ocean depths. Soon Rose's bubble broke the surface of the water near the shore where Joseph, Wisher, and Snowflake waited in their camp. She looked back toward the ocean just in time to see the king dive back into the waves with powerful flip of his tail.

Rose exited the bubble and waded toward the shore, waving to her companions. Joseph ran from the beach and splashed through the water. He stopped, holding his eyes against the glimmering light reflecting off the golden garment in Rose's hands.

"I take it all went well?" he asked.

Rose patted the folded shirt she held against her breast. "All went well," she replied. "Am I in time for dinner? I will eat anything but fish."

Chapter Ten

Rose sighed in frustration as she clutched the golden shirt. The markings the mermaid princess saw were impossible to look at in the open sunlight. The brilliance of the shirt's reflection was blinding, and the markings seemed to vanish when the clouds darkened the sky. Joseph attempted to examine the shirt underwater as the mermaid had done but could not see any outstanding pattern in the weavings.

"You are certain there is a hidden pattern in it?" Joseph asked as he shook seawater from his ears.

Rose turned the garment over in her hands, her eyes squinting as the sun shone off it. "I know there is. The princess saw. I could even…"

Rose paused and looked off to the waves crashing before the shore. Quietly she closed her eyes and placed her hands on the golden fibers. Joseph and Snowflake watched in silence as she moved her hand over the back of the shirt slowly. After a moment, she began to trace something unseen with her fingers.

"Here. Here is Ametheria. I can feel the palace nestled in its hills and valleys. The cottage we began our journey is here with the path running to the road which runs to the river town. There. There is where we met Snowflake. Now to Jagged Mountain...,"

Rose jerked her hand away as if stuck by a pin.

"Lives up to its name, it does. Now to where we met the old woman. Now to the shore. Wait. Wait...there. There it is. A path. No. A road? A long, long road leading to...a town? A town by a large space. It moves and ebbs. The ocean! A harbor town. I feel...,"

Rose burst into sudden, surprised laughter.

"A ship! A ship moving on the sea! To where? A large land mass. Not an island. A country due south. A flat country. Barren. Warm. Dry."

Rose opened her eyes.

"A desert," she said. "We are traveling to a desert country."

A few weeks later, Rose and her companions caught sight of a harbor town nestled in a large cove. The evening before entering the town, Rose and Joseph discussed in great detail establishing identities as sister and brother since a non-related couple of their age would have found trouble gaining passage on any ship. They laid out their story of meeting their parents at their destination and even took pains to distress their already modest clothes to distance their appearance from royalty as far as possible. All the work seemed to be for nothing as hours passed after riding into town and they had yet to succeed in booking passage on any ship.

As Joseph thanked a crew member of a small sailing vessel for checking on available cabins, Rose looked down the harbor for any other passenger ships. The only remaining ship at the end of the docks was a modest cargo vessel named Savanna.

"Looks like we may have to find lodging for a while," Joseph said as he walked up to Rose. "That was the last passenger ship and they, too, have no available cabins."

"What about a cargo ship?" Rose asked pointing to the Savanna.

Joseph frowned at the sight of the ship. "No. From what I understand, cargo vessels need crew members, not mere passengers."

"Then let us join their crew."

"That might be a problem," Joseph said looking around. "I do not see any women crew members on any of these ships."

But Rose wasn't listening. She was already approaching a bearded man who was busy ordering the Savanna's crew to load crates on the ship.

"I beg your pardon, sir," Rose said to the man.

"One moment, lass," the man replied and turned his attention back to the work in front of him. "I told ya' lads to put the large crates in first, then the barrels and *then* the small crates! We're due out before nightfall or the captain will have to pay another gold piece to the dock master for stayin' over. And guess who's pay that's coming out of?"

Shaking his head, the man turned his attention back to Rose and Joseph, who had now joined her. "Alcott Goody, First Mate of the Savanna at your service. What can I do, for ya'?"

"We are looking for passage for ourselves and our stallion on a ship travelling to a country due south of here," Joseph said.

"Aye, we're headin' that way," the first mate said as he looked from Joseph to Rose. "Ya' married?"

"No, sir." Rose replied. "I am his sister."

"Ya' don't look it."

"She takes after our mother. I resemble our father," Joseph answered.

"If ya' says so," Alcott replied. "Ya' looked far too young to be wed. We do have room for ya,' if ya' have the coin for it."

"Is there no means by which we can work for our passage?" Rose asked.

"We have enough deck hands, Missy," the first mate said. "More than enough as it is. We have no more room for crew."

"Besides money, is there anything else your ship needs that we may try and provide for trade?" asked Joseph.

The first mate stroked his reddish-brown beard in thought. "Wait 'ere a moment," he said and walked over to the edge of the dock where the cargo was being hoisted into the ship's hold. After some minutes speaking with a crew member, who appeared to be cataloging supplies and cargo, the first mate returned.

"I do not think ya' can help us, but since ya' inquired, we have not found enough salt to partake on our journey."

"Salt?" Rose asked.

"To preserve some of the rations for the months ahead on the sea," Joseph said.

"Good guess for a landlubber," the first mate said with a crooked grin and a pat on Joseph's shoulder. "Ya' bring me two barrels of salt, and ya' shall have yer beds on the ship."

"Salt is rather rare, sir." Rose said. "It more treasured in parts of the world than gold." Rose caught sight of Joseph looking at her with raised eyebrows. "So I have heard," she quickly added.

"Ya' asked, so's I told ya'. There is a merchant who is to meet us here in three hours who promises the salt we need but for more than we can afford to pay. We'll have to trade some of our other supplies—likely our wine—in order to pay for it and that would make for a miserable time at sea. Get us the salt, and ya' will make our journey much more bearable."

Rose and Joseph left Alcott to his duties and walked behind a nearby supply house where Snowflake and Wisher waited.

"So, where does that leave us?" Joseph asked.

"This is the only offer we have been able to receive," Rose said. "Once they leave, there may not be another opportunity arrive for weeks."

"It does not make much difference," Joseph said with a shrug. "We have no more salt than we have money."

Rose frowned. Joseph was correct. She walked over to Wisher and patted him. He snorted and uttered a low whinny, a sign of hunger. Rose opened the large sack tied to their supply bundle, reached in, and took out a green apple as fresh as if it had been just picked from a tree.

"Here you go, boy," she said as Wisher carefully took the apple from his mistress. Suddenly, a thought struck Rose. "Joseph, would you consider salt *food*?"

"No," Joseph said. "An ingredient, perhaps."

Rose unbundled the sack and laid it upside down on the ground. She pulled the mouth of the sack, now facing the ground, out as wide as it would go. She then clutched the bottom of the sack and pulled upward.

Joseph's jaw hung agape as the sack lifted from the ground. As the mouth of the sack raised, the iron rims and wooden planks of a barrel appeared underneath. The mouth of the sack grew tighter around the widening barrel as it slid and, for a moment, became stuck around the middle. Then, with a *whhhoooooooppp*-ing sound, popped free revealing a full barrel two-thirds Joseph's height.

Joseph approached the barrel as Rose worked the cork in the top loose. The cork soon came free, and Rose stuck her hand in. When she removed it, she clutched a handful of crystalline, white grains.

"I think ingredients work," Rose said with a smile.

A coughing was heard from behind. Rose and Joseph turned to see in the shadows of a neighboring building a large man leaning against a wall. His face was half hidden by the large brim of a ratty hat sitting crookedly on his head; a mop of long, tangled black hair twisting out from underneath and a beard as thick and dark as smoke hid the rest of his features. In one hand he held a bottle and the other rested against a sheathed cutlass. The man regarded them for a moment, lifted the bottle to his lips and drank. He then smiled at them and Rose noticed, even in the shadows, every tooth in his mouth was gold. With a tip of his hat, the man walked away and disappeared around the corner of the building.

"Do you think he saw?" Joseph asked.

"Undoubtedly," Rose replied. "But he is likely to think it is his brain swimming in rum making him see things. Regardless, we should be off soon."

A few minutes later, the first mate of the Savanna stared at the handful of salt Rose produced from one of the two barrels she stood beside. "Never in my days have I seen such purity," he said in a whisper.

91

"And we thank you in advance for a smooth and safe journey, sir," Rose said.

Alcott laughed every bit of the way as he and Joseph rolled the barrels to the loading dock. As the first mate announced the two new passengers and the cargo they provided, a cheer went up, and Rose and Joseph suddenly found themselves well-received by twenty new friends.

Chapter Eleven

Rose awoke in her cabin with a start. She kept still and listened. All was silent, but she could sense a presence with her in the dark. "Show yourself—"

A hand suddenly clamped on her mouth.

"Shhhh," whispered Joseph. He gently removed his hand.

"Joseph, what is the meaning of this?" Rose quietly demanded. "What are you doing in my cabin?"

Joseph did not respond. After a moment, Rose realized he was straining to listen to sounds she was now hearing herself. Somewhere from the deck a couple of levels above them, the sounds of footfalls and muffled shouting leaked through the boards.

"We are in trouble," Joseph said.

Rose jumped from her bed and grabbed her garments. "Is it a mutiny?" Rose asked, though she doubted the answer would be 'yes.' Since the launching of the ship a week ago, Rose had enjoyed being in the company of a brotherhood of shipmates as close as the ones on the Savanna. Any troubles between them often passed quickly and laughed about for hours afterward.

"No," Joseph said. From the sound of his voice, he had turned his head away from Rose, and she dressed, though he would not have been able to see her in the dark. "It was the jostling of the other ship scraping against us that woke me. I am surprised you slept through it."

"Pirates?"

"I believe so, yes. I have sent a spy upward to confirm my suspicions."

"A spy? But how—" Rose's asked but an odd noise coming from the cabin door stopped her: a slight, scratching sound. Before Rose could object, she heard Joseph step toward the door and open it. Rose could make out a small shape close to the floor enter the room.

"I cannot see all of them, sir," Snowflake said, "but there are at least fifteen. And their captain is a sizable beast, I must say. A frightful giant."

"What do we do?" Rose asked.

"As far as I can see it, we have two choices," Joseph said. "We stay hidden here and hope they do not make their way down to the cabins..."

"Little ones!" a voice boomed from overhead. Even through two levels of the ship, the voice sounded like its owner was standing in the dark next to them. "Come out, ye brats, before I begin feedin' your friends to the sharks!"

"...or we can go up and see what has happened." Joseph said.

Rose picked up Snowflake and placed him on her pillow. "Stay here and stay quiet."

"You do not have to tell me twice, Princess," the cat replied.

Quietly, Rose and Joseph left the shelter of the cabin and made their way to the upper level of the ship just beneath the deck. Not a living soul—shipmate or pirate—was below deck.

"They know we have nowhere to go," Rose said.

"Yes," Joseph confirmed, "they can afford to wait for us to come to them."

Rose and Joseph approached the steep stairway leading to a trapdoor in the deck above. They looked at each other one final time before mounting the steps.

The door above suddenly swung outward, and they found themselves staring straight into the points of seven cutlasses. Among the scowling, unkempt pirate crew stood a tall, broad man with a thick, dark beard and long, black hair. Within the coarse hair was a grin, and within that grin gleamed a mouthful of solid gold teeth.

"We've been a waitin' fer ya' young-uns," the man said. He removed his hat and took a mocking bow. "I am Captain Gold Tooth of the ship Dragonslayer, and ye be my prisoners."

In seconds, rough hands had seized Rose and Joseph and pulled them to the deck. Joseph struggled but was quickly kicked in the lower back, and he fell crashing to the deck planks.

"Vermin!" Rose cried as she wrenched free from the pirates and knelt next to her friend. Captain Gold Tooth laughed long and loud at the sight before them.

"I am all right, Rose," Joseph said through clenched teeth. "Been kicked worse by a frightened horse."

Rose helped Joseph to his feet. She glanced around at the filthy crew surrounding them. She quickly counted seventeen pirates on the deck of the Savanna before her eyes caught sight of a massive shape beside their boat.

The pirate ship sat motionless on the ocean waters, which only added to its terrifying appearance. Its hull, deck and even the sails were dark and would be near impossible to see even in a moonlit night. Rose could imagine the terror of a ship's crew when they would catch sight of this shadow of the sea pulling alongside them, for by the time they could see it, it would be too late.

Rose shook off any feelings of dread and glared at the pirate captain. "Where are the others? The crew that served this ship. Where are they?"

Captain Gold Tooth raised an eyebrow and smirked. "Why, I ain't harmed a hair on their little heads, miss. See for yourself."

The pirate crew parted and revealed the bound and gagged forms of the Savanna's crew piled in a corner of the deck of the ship.

Enraged, Rose opened her mouth to speak, but a sudden, strong grip on her wrist made her stop. She turned and saw Joseph staring into her eyes. Rose took his meaning immediately. She had been dangerously close to dropping her disguised mannerisms of a common woman and reverting to that of royalty, making an already dangerous situation worse. Her face reddened, but she closed her mouth as Joseph opened his.

"What are your intentions toward us, Captain?"

"Why, I just had a wish to be neighborly and stop by to say hello to ya's," Gold Tooth replied, his poor humor getting everything from chuckles to guffaws from his crew. "But I see no reason to continue with pleasantries while my prize awaits. I hear tell…"

Suddenly, a loud whinny cut through the night as Wisher appeared on deck, bound by heavy ropes and being pulled along by two of the pirates.

"Wisher!" Rose cried, unable to contain herself. A loud chorus of laughter erupted from the pirate crew at her outburst.

"Take 'im over to the Dragonslayer, gents!" Gold Tooth bellowed. "E'll bring a few coppers at port if we don't eat 'im first!"

"Monster!" Rose yelled at the captain as Wisher, fighting against his captors, was led across a wide set of planks, and he soon disappeared into the cargo hold of the pirate ship. Gold Tooth's attention returned to his young captors.

"Now then, where were we? Ah, yes! The magic sack in yer possession, boy. The one that produces barrels of salt from thin air."

Rose and Joseph froze, and before either could catch themselves, they simultaneously spoke. "What sack?"

Gold Tooth's grin grew wider. "'What sack,' indeed." The pirate captain nodded to his crew, and in moments, one of the Savanna's deckhands found himself dangling over the deep, dark waters of the sea by his ankles.

"Hold, Captain," Joseph said. "There is no need for that. I will retrieve what you came here for."

Rose watched as two pirates approached and stood at each side of Joseph as the deck hand was tossed back to the safety of the ship's deck. Gold Tooth eyed Joseph. "Be quick about it, lad, or you'll be hearin' a lot of bodies goin' over the side."

Rose saw Joseph give her a smile as he started toward the trap door to the hold of the ship. But before he could take the first step down into the darkness, she said, "So, you claim to be the terrible pirate Gold Tooth. Is that it?" Joseph turned, his eyes wide and brows raised at Rose's sudden outburst.

"They call me terrible!" he said. "I can think of a lot of worse things to be called, eh lads?" The pirate's laughter filled the air until Rose's next words cut through it like a sword.

"Smelly, oafish, and cowardly would be more accurate, I would say."

The night became instantly quiet. For the first time since boarding the Savanna, Gold Tooth's smile left his face. "I beg yer pardon, miss," he said in an even, measured tone.

"You cannot be the famed pirate captain Gold Tooth," Rose continued, unwavering. "Even I have heard of his deeds, and you, a portly glob of a man, who would bully his way to a prize than win one....well, you sir, are no Captain Gold Tooth."

The conviction in Rose's voice was without question or hesitation, and for the first time, the captain seemed to be at a loss for words. But Rose saw the clenching of the captain's fists, and she knew Gold Tooth was on the verge of a furious act.

"No one, especially a girl, has ever spoken to me that way an' lived," Gold Tooth said through a jaw so tight the gold teeth sparked with friction.

"Cutting down a defenseless girl in front of your crew is your way of proving to them who you are? The terrible pirate Captain Gold Tooth is a master of the cutlass, but I wager you could not best any man on this ship in a fair fight."

In a blur of movement, Gold Tooth's cutlass was out of its sheath. "Choose the one ya' wish to die, girl, and know their blood will be on ya' hands."

"My brother."

A smattering of astonished laughter rippled through the pirate crew. The captain looked over at Joseph and chuckled. "I'll slice 'im to ribbons in seconds. Why don't you choose someone with a fairer chance?"

"Are you backing down, dear Captain?" Rose boldly asked. "I'll wager this 'magic sack' you seem so fit to take from us that you cannot best my brother in a fair duel."

The pirate captain was silent, his eyes quickly glancing around in a brief uncertainty but clenched his jaw. "I accept."

Joseph was pulled away from the hold's entrance and pushed into the center of the deck facing the furious glare of his opponent. One of the pirates unsheathed his sword to hand to Joseph.

"At least give me a moment to say farewell to my dear brother, Captain." Rose said.

Gold Tooth nodded and Joseph was shoved over to Rose. She embraced Joseph and whispered in his ear, "My parents trained you in fencing, yes?" Worry cracked her voice for the first time since the ordeal had begun.

"Yes," Joseph replied. "That they did."

"Give me ten minutes, then cut the prisoners free when the pirates are distracted."

"Ten? Rose, a duel lasts less than a minute, maybe a minute and a half, at most. Why ten?"

"I am going to get my horse back."

Growing restless, the pirates pulled Joseph away from Rose and stuck the handle of the waiting cutlass in his hand. With a fierce howl, Gold Tooth charged across the deck of the ship before Joseph had a chance to turn and face his opponent. With no option of defense, Joseph tucked his body and rolled away from Gold Tooth's attack. The pirate's cutlass sliced through the air at the young man, but now Joseph was on the ready. He raised his sword, and the two blades met in the air with a spark that raised a cheer from the pirates. In seconds, steel clashed with steel and the fight began to rage across the deck of the ship.

Rose watched, but not the fight. She observed the attention of the pirate crew growing more and more focused on the fight their captain was furiously engaged in. As the battle continued well beyond the point of most duels, the entire crew whooped and howled in a frenzy. Quietly, Rose crept away in the darkness. Removing her shoes, Rose mounted the planks connecting the vessels and was on the deck of the Dragonslayer in seconds.

Rapid footfalls ascended the steps leading from the ship's hold to the deck, and Rose quickly hid behind one of the ship's cannons as two pirates appeared three feet from her hiding place.

"Who's he fightin'?" one of them asked.

"Can't tell from here," the other said. "Let's go have a look see."

"What about the horse?"

"Ah, he's tied and bolted away. He ain't goin' nowhere. C'mon, ya' girl."

The two pirates ran across the planks. Rose emerged from her hiding place and hurried down the ramp into the blackness of the hold.

Rose stood for a moment and listened. She could hear no voices or sounds of any other people in the dark. Feeling around, Rose found an oil lantern hanging from a nail. She found a stone and flint nearby and lit the lantern. Shadows danced across the walls of the ship's belly as Rose began her search.

"Wisher?" Rose called out in a low voice. "Wisher, boy? Wisher?"

From behind a bolted door in the back of the hold, the low whinny of a horse echoed, and Rose rushed over. "Wisher? Answer me, boy."

Rose heard another whinny and she quickly grabbed the bolt of the door to slide it back. From the darkness behind Rose, a hand shot out and grasped her arm. Rose spun around, and she stared at the leering face of one of the pirates.

"Well, now, what have I got here?" the pirate said.

Chapter Twelve

"I'll say ya"ll fetch more coin than the nag," the grinning pirate said as he pulled Rose away from the storeroom where Wisher was held. Rose struggled fiercely as the pirate gripped her wrist and led her to the ship's wall where sets of chains and shackles hung from iron bolts. As the pirate reached for one of the shackles, Rose twisted in his grip and drove a knee into his stomach. Rank breath rushed from the pirate's lungs as he collapsed to the floor. Rose turned to run to the bolted storeroom but was suddenly grabbed from behind and lifted from the floor. Rose let a shrill cry as the pirate slammed her downward on the wooden planks.

A loud thud rocked the storeroom door.

The pirate bent down to grab Rose by the throat and drag her back to the iron shackles. Rose thrust her foot upward and caught the pirate with a glancing blow to the jaw. The pirate reached down and slapped Rose across the face.

Another loud thud slammed from the storeroom door as the wood in it cracked.

Rose tried to blink the tears from her eyes as she lashed out at her attacker. Warding off her blows, the pirate grabbed Rose by the hair and pulled her to the wall. Rose shrieked as the pirate grabbed one of the chained shackles and pulled one of her wrists to it.

Suddenly, the storeroom door erupted outward. Thunderous hoof beats echoed in the ship as the pirate turned to see two fiery eyes in a blur of white racing toward him. The pirate opened his mouth to yell but was cut short as Wisher drove headlong into him, sending him sailing backward into a support beam. He fell to the floor of the hold, motionless.

Rose stood as Wisher turned toward her, and what she saw tore her heart in two. The white hair on the horse's forehead was lined with red streaks. He had broken the door down by ramming straight against it. On his sides were raw marks where his rope bonds had ripped against him when he tore free. Weeping, Rose held Wisher by the neck and stroked his mane.

"My poor friend," she whispered. "My poor, poor friend."

Wisher uttered a soft whinny and gently nuzzled Rose's reddening cheek. The two comforted each other as the sounds of swords clashing and cheers drifted outside. Rose straightened and looked toward the opening above. Her jaw clenched, she quickly walked over to the fallen pirate, took his cutlass and mounted her horse.

"Carry me with you," she said and Wisher charged up the hold's ramp.

Rose turned Wisher in the direction of the Savanna. Even from the distance between her and the deck of the other ship, she could see Joseph's tired arms as they blocked each of Gold Tooth's blows, each clash of the swords seeming to weaken them more.

Rose gave Wisher a slight, but firm, kick to the side and the horse took off to the plank walkway connecting the ships. She bellowed in rage and raised her cutlass in the air as Wisher charged over the boards, his hooves stomping like thunder.

The Dragonslayer's crew scattered, their faces etched in fear and shock, as Wisher leaped and landed on the deck next to Gold Tooth. Rose kicked outward and stuck the pirate captain in the face, knocking him flat on his back. Joseph, his body drooping in weariness, crossed the deck and set to freeing the Savanna's crew.

Recovering from their surprise, the pirates rushed at Rose and Wisher but could not get close enough to the princess or her steed. They were continuously kicked by the beating hooves or sliced by the whirring sword, driving them away. Within moments, the pirates were set upon by a new problem, the freed members of the Savanna's crew as they joined the fight.

Rose gave Wisher a kick, and the horse charged through the fighting men, scattering pirates over the deck. A group of them began crossing the planks connecting the two ships. Rose knew if any got on board the Dragonslayer, they would fire the cannons on the pirate vessel and send the Savanna to the bottom of the ocean. Rose quickly drove Wisher toward the planks and reared him upward. Wisher's front hooves kicked outward and knocked the planks from the side of the Savanna, sending them and the crossing pirates splashing down into the water below.

Turning back to the battle on the Savanna's deck, Rose looked through the men as the Savanna's crew began rounding up the defeated pirates, binding them with ropes. Rose began to grow cold with fear. She could not see Joseph. A clatter of swords sounded from the stern of the ship, and Rose finally spotted him by the ship's helm, once again engaged in a duel with Captain Gold Tooth.

Now, it was the pirate captain that seemed to be tiring, his legs trembling and his arms drooping, while Joseph battled on, wearing his enemy down. Each strike of Gold Tooth's sword was met with Joseph's, the feared pirate backing away toward the stern of the ship. In a sudden burst of energy, Gold Tooth leaped forward with a mighty swing of his sword and Joseph gracefully tucked and rolled on his back as the pirate captain reached him. He then thrust his legs upward and sent Gold Tooth flying into the air and crashing down onto the main deck.

Rose looked down at the once-fearsome man as Gold Tooth started to pull himself to his feet. She turned Wisher around, his backside facing the pirate captain as he stood up, and dismounted.

"Wisher wanted to thank you for your hospitality," Rose said, giving the horse a swift pat. Wisher's hind legs rose up and kicked Gold Tooth square in the chest, sending him sailing out and away from the Savanna. He bounced off the side of the Dragonslayer before splashing into the water below.

A loud cheer burst from the Savanna's crew, congratulations given all around. Many hands clapped Joseph on the back as he came down from the stern of the ship. Pausing, Joseph bent down and picked a tiny object off the deck before walking over to Rose. The two friends embraced and sat down as the crew of the Savanna fished out the overboard pirates and bound them

105

with their shipmates. Joseph and Rose looked up at the stars as they shone over the ocean. Without speaking, Joseph took Rose's hand and placed something in it.

"What is this?" she asked.

"Not much, but it is the best I can do for a birthday present."

"Birth…?" Rose started and then smirked. She shook her head at the thought of two years and adventures past. Finally, she looked down at her hand and laughed. After a moment, she and Joseph laughed together on the deck of the Savanna as a single, shiny gold tooth rested in her palm.

Chapter Thirteen

"Rose, wake up."

Rose's eyelids fluttered once before slowly opening. Her brow furrowed as she squinted against the brightness all around her. Joseph knelt above her and moved to shield the sun from her eyes. He slipped a hand gently under her neck and tilted her head upward.

"You need to drink. Please," he said as he placed a leather pouch to her lips. Rose drank rapidly until the pouch was dry. Feeling strength returning to her body, she sat up.

"Was I asleep? I do not remember stopping."

"You were on the verge of collapse. You do not remember almost tumbling from Wisher's back?"

Rose shook her head.

"This heat; it's monstrous," Joseph said as he looked about their barren surroundings. "I never knew there could be heat such as this."

"We are drying out like spring flowers in the summer," Snowflake said as he sat upon Wisher's haunches, his tongue jutting from his mouth.

Rose stood and brushed the dust from her clothes. "We must keep ourselves more refreshed than usual, I expect."

Joseph motioned to a distant outcropping of rock. "Let us journey there. I expect we will find shade from the sun for the day, and we can work on getting ourselves healthy for another day's journey."

Rose didn't argue. Though she wanted to continue her quest, she had never felt as weak as she did now. "Get more water from the sack to fill the pouch. We will walk alongside Wisher."

"Rose...."

"No arguments, Joseph. Wisher is suffering as we are, maybe more so. We shall not ride on him as long as we are in this oppressive heat."

"Ah, Princess..." began Snowflake.

"Yes, cat, you can stay up there."

"Many thanks, Your Highness. That hot, dusty ground makes my paws a little crispy."

In less than an hour, Rose, Joseph, Snowflake, and Wisher reached the relatively cool shade. Joseph sat against the rock wall, his eyes closed. Rose patted Wisher's nose as he took an apple from her hand.

"We will need to make camp shortly," Rose said.

Joseph nodded. It was startling how cold the nights became in this land. "I dare say, I see not one tree or even twig to make a fire tonight. We will have to bundle ourselves."

Rose rubbed her eyes, sore from the bright surroundings. She sat beside Joseph and laid her head on his shoulder, a sigh escaping her lips.

"Worried?' Joseph asked.

"Weary. I do not think I have ever been so tired. My entire body feels lifeless." A moment of silence passed. "I want to go home. I want to see my sisters again. I want to see the kingdom's lush fields and hills. I want to feel the wind against me as I ride Wisher through the courtyard. I want to hear my father's voice cheering for me.

"I want to see my mother."

The two friends held each other in the shade. As the sun slipped over the horizon, they silently set up camp. During the night, Rose looked upward at the clearest sky she had ever seen as she lay on the desert floor, and she wondered if her mother could see the same stars as her. Finally, she slept.

Rose stood in her golden coronation gown, motionless in a dying land. Thick, dry brambles covered the once lush, green earth. The hills blanketed in rotting, dead trees as the wind whistled through the empty, crumbling homes. And, in the distance, stood the ruins of her palace.

The people of her homeland trudged through the horrifying scene, thin with starvation. Accusing eyes in sunken sockets glared at Rose and her fancy clothing. She tried calling to them, but no sound escaped her throat. She ran to them, arms extended in an act of comfort, but she passed through the people like ghosts. She tried to scream, to plead, to beg forgiveness.

They cannot hear you, child, a voice said.

Rose turned and saw the form of her mother: thin, grey, and dressed in rags. Her lips and eyes held no cheer for her firstborn. Her once lustrous auburn hair had thinned and had begun to fall out. Her cheeks were pale and sunken, and Rose knew she was dying. She cried for her mother and tried to run to her but found she could not.

It's too late, Rose, her mother said, eyes full of sorrow. Too late.

Silently, Rose begged her mother to tell her what happened. Rose's mother looked at her daughter.

You gave up, she said.

Rose stifled a scream as she sat upright in the cold night of the desert. The blanket violently flung from her during the dream, and now, the chill of the air clung to the sweat covering her, and she shuttered, as much from the dream as the cold.

You gave up, her mother had said.

Something in the darkness touched Rose's shoulder, and she turned. Wisher nuzzled against her. He lowered his head and pushed her blanket toward her. Rose picked it up and wrapped it back around herself. She stroked Wisher's muzzle. "You have come so far with me, have you not?" she asked. "You have suffered so much for me."

Wisher gave a sympathetic nicker and nuzzled again.

"I wish *you* could speak. You know me, perhaps better than anyone would, my friend. I cannot help but wonder if Mother had her times of doubt on her journey. I wish she could have told me about it."

110

Wisher uttered another soft snort. She smiled in return; a tired smile, but one of renewed strength.

"I am fine now, my friend," she said, giving his muzzle a playful scratch. "Thank you for asking."

Rose wrapped herself tightly in the blanket and lay back down. She listened to the gentle music of the desert insects and fell asleep.

It was another three days of walking before Rose and Joseph spied their destination in the distance. A canyon wound through the desert floor like a great snake cutting deeply into the earth. It was a grand sight, and the travelers gazed at it for a long time.

"The sights we have seen," Joseph said. "By God, they are beautiful."

Rose didn't answer, but the wondrous look in her eyes agreed fully.

By late afternoon, Rose and Joseph had come within a hundred yards of the canyon's edge. Rose marveled at the various colors of earth and rock that comprised the inner walls of the canyon. Snowflake, however, seemed not as much impressed with the gaping hole they approached as evidenced by the fur standing straight up on his back. He growled as he sat in the saddle, and Rose laughed to herself as she stroked him in comfort. As they neared the edge, Joseph held a hand out to Rose to stop as he walked on ahead. Rose held Wisher back from the edge as Joseph took careful steps and peered into the canyon. He turned to Rose with a broad grin and motioned for her to come forward.

"Stay, Wisher," Rose said in a firm voice, and she left him and Snowflake to join Joseph's side. Wisher snorted once and took one step forward.

"You heard Her Highness, you overgrown mule. Stay," Snowflake said with a hint of irritation. Wisher gave the cat a short, annoyed grunt and stood still.

Rose neared the edge of the canyon and held out her hand for Joseph to take it. Slowly, Rose leaned over and looked to the canyon floor. A slight gasp left Rose's lips as she saw a clear, shining river below. The water flowed steadily along the winding canyon, and lining the banks of the river was lush greenery and towering trees. Even from the height of the canyon's roof, Rose could hear songbirds singing below.

"I dare say," said Joseph, "we are long due for a bathing."

It took most of the day, but as the sun set, Rose and Joseph found a path down the side of the canyon they could comfortably travel. They camped by the start of the path, and in the morning light, they walked to the bottom. The canyon walls seemed impossibly tall—much taller than three castle towers standing end to end. After finding a comfortable place to rest and lunch, Rose bathed and washed some of her garments as Joseph journeyed a little farther down the river's edge. After that, Rose and Snowflake sat behind the cover of some bushes and talked as Joseph bathed. At some points of the conversation, Rose would break off and shout teases over the greenery to Joseph, trying to embarrass him. Later, as their garments dried in the midday sun, Joseph and Rose played dice, while the animals rested under the shade of the surrounding trees.

"How far does the canyon stretch?" Rose asked.

"Oh," he said looking down the canyon, "I would say five leagues, maybe eight. Do not distract me now." Joseph rolled the dice and winced at the terrible set of numbers that came up. Rose scooped up the dice.

"Did you see anything on your walk?"

"No, but there seems to be a path that follows the river. It is so unused and overgrown, I cannot say if it is man or creature made." Joseph winced again as Rose rolled a powerful set of numbers. "I do so wish we would have had the mind to bring cards. Dice was never my game of skill."

Rose smirked. "You must not feel bad. The only ones who can best me in dice are Daisy and our family's holy man."

"You must miss it."

Rose smiled at Joseph warmly but also in sullen agreement.

"What do you think it will be like?" Joseph asked. "Being a queen?"

"I have not really considered it, now that you ask. I suspect not much different than being a princess. Oh, I will have much more responsibilities for the well-being of my subjects, but I imagine it will not be much different to how I lived before."

"I wonder."

"What?"

"Do you think *we* will be the same? Our friendship, I mean."

"Well...of course. Why not?"

"Queens do not play dice with stable boys."

Rose began to say something but stopped for lack of an answer. They played the rest of the game in silence.

The following day, Rose and Joseph traveled along the river, both riding on Wisher in the cool air of the canyon. The stillness of their surroundings commanded silence, and neither of them spoke until just after noon when Joseph said, "I think we are here."

Rose looked ahead, but the branches from a tree obstructed most of her view, so she dismounted, and Joseph following suit. Rose stepped forward from under the tree, squinting her eyes against the glare of the sun.

The canyon walls spread apart before Rose and Joseph and curved around, connecting to form the canyon's end. Filling the grand circle was a fishing village. The canyon river cut neatly through the center of the village where many odd-looking buildings had been erected. Spread out to the ends of the canyon were dwellings and a few farms. The dwellings nestled in the shade provided by the canyon walls, while the farms more centrally located to catch the sunshine. And in the back of the canyon enclosure was a palace unlike any Rose had ever seen before. The palace was carved into the rock wall of the canyon's end and stretched almost to the top. The face of the palace was decorated in ornate carvings. Rose noticed that whatever stonecutters had created this wondrous palace had even used the colorful layers of rock to accent many carvings and, judging by the windows, had they even separated the floors of the palace by them. And in the front, a wide opening had been cut to allow the river to run into the palace.

"It is beautiful," Rose said.

"I should hope so. It took the better part of twenty years to chisel it, or so I'm told," a voice said from behind them.

Rose and Joseph spun around to see a handsome young man standing on the trail behind them. By Rose's estimation he was the same age as she or just a year older. He wore unusually long pants that came up to his ribs, a thin, white shirt and barefoot, holding his shoes and stockings in one hand. His other held a net with a heavy amount of fish. He was also soaking wet.

"I didn't mean to startle you, but I figured you were going to stand and stare all day, and I needed by," the man said.

"Oh, my apologies," Rose replied as she and Joseph stepped aside.

"Much obliged," the man said as he walked past.

"If I may, what place is this?" Rose asked.

"Sorry, I forget my manners; my mother says it's my biggest fault. This is the humble Kingdom of Engelbrecht."

"'Engel...*brecht*?' Is that right?" Joseph said.

"Yes," the man replied. "It's named after the family that has ruled the land since its foundation. Nice enough people but darn ugly. Their two kids are a horrendous sight."

Rose was a bit taken aback by the man's bluntness. "Oh...well...thank you for your kindness in speaking with us."

"My pleasure. We of Engelbrecht keep to ourselves, so to chat with strangers is a nice change, even ones who talk a little funny." With a friendly wink and a smile, the man turned and started down the path, whistling a merry tune. Rose and Joseph looked at each other, shrugged, and followed.

"What is so funny about the manner in which we speak?" Joseph asked Rose.

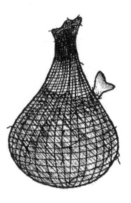

Chapter Fourteen

"So, where are you from?" the young man asked as he led Rose and her company through the center of the village. The odor of fish was strong, and Snowflake had to be restrained on several occasions. Many of the residents were too busy working the fishing nets by the river to take notice of the strangers in their midst. Those who did, looked at them with a mix of curiosity and mild suspicion, but as soon as they saw the young man with them, they immediately warmed, and some even waved in a casual manner. Rose noticed that the young ladies were particularly happy if the man smiled and waved back.

"We hail from Ametheria," Rose said. "It is a kingdom across the ocean."

"Ametheria?" the man said scratching his chin in thought. "Have your people traveled through here before?"

"We have had no expeditions across the sea, to my knowledge. Why do you ask?"

"Oh, I seem to recall hearing stories about someone from your kingdom visiting here many years ago. As I said, we keep to ourselves, so travelers are few and far between. I can't seem to remember the circumstance, though."

Rose and Joseph glanced at each other. For the moment, they were as puzzled as their companion.

"I take it fishing is your main trade?" Rose asked.

The man laughed. "How can you tell? Smells wonderful, doesn't it? You do get used to it quickly. In fact, any time I go upriver away from the village, I almost miss the....excuse me a moment."

The man had looked upward to a platform where several men hauled in a massive catch. He reached into his net, pulled out a speckled fish the size of his forearm, and, to Rose's surprise, slung the fish upward, and it slapped against the hindquarters of one of the workers with a loud pop. The worker yelped with surprise and turned around to face his attacker. Upon seeing the young man below, he scowled.

"Edwin Cromwell! You've been upriver poaching again!" he shouted, pointing an accusing finger downward in a dramatic, almost comical, manner.

"With your fishing skills, Rauf, I have to or the whole village would starve," the man, now known as Edwin, shouted back.

With a loud yell, the worker leaped from the platform toward Edwin, and in an instant, the two men tumbled in the dirt. All the workers immediately ceased what they were doing and cheered as the two men wrestled.

Rose watched the spectacle in uncomfortable silence. Edwin, the smaller of the two men, managed to twist around in his opponent's grip and pin one shoulder to the ground. However, his opponent shoved him away and before he could recover, he found Rauf sitting squarely on his back. Edwin squirmed helplessly against the larger Rauf, unsuccessful at bucking him off. The crowd laughed at the helpless lad on the ground, and that laughter grew into a hysteria as Rauf slapped Edwin in the face with his own fish.

"Hey! Unfair!" Edwin cried out.

Rose grimaced at the sight and turned to Joseph. "Why do you not put an end to this?"

"An end to what? They are just having some sport, is all."

"He is being tormented."

"He is laughing is what he is doing," Joseph said, pointing. Rose looked closer and could see that Edwin was, indeed, laughing right along with the rest of the spectators. Rose rolled her eyes and made a silent curse at the male gender.

"That is enough!" a voice bellowed, and the entire village immediately silenced.

Rauf leaped to his feet and quickly pulled Edwin to his. They brushed themselves off as a burly, bearded man stomped over to them. "Why is it we cannot go a week here without you two getting into mischief? Rauf, you just about lost that catch so you could fool around. And you, Edwin! Either take your fish and go home, or grab a net and give us a hand. What do you say?"

"I will take the first choice, sir," Edwin said.

"That's what I thought. Rauf, you go home too and get changed. You've torn the seat of your trousers clean off, and if you dawdle, I'll have a great mind to make you fish without a stitch on!"

"Yes, sir," Rauf said as he and Edwin hurried away.

Unsure of what else to do, Rose and Joseph followed.

As the group hurried away, Rose heard the burly man shout from behind, "And no more foolishness during work time! I don't care if you are Her Highness's sons!"

"You didn't tell them?" Rauf asked his younger brother with a slight punch to the shoulder.

"I don't see new people all that often. It didn't occur to me."

Rauf rolled his eyes at his brother and turned to Rose and Joseph with a bow. "I apologize for my brother's rudeness in not making the proper introductions. That is his biggest fault, or so our mother says."

"Yes, I have heard," Rose replied, looking at Edwin with narrow eyes. To her surprise, the young man blushed and looked away.

"I am Prince Rauf Humphrey Engelbrecht, first son of King Gregory Cromwell Engelbrecht and Queen Margaret Rose Engelbrecht," Rauf said with a bow.

"And I am Prince Edwin Cromwell Engelbrecht, second son of King Gregory Cromwell Engelbrecht and Queen Margaret Rose Engelbrecht." In one motion, Edwin bowed, took Rose's hand, and kissed it. His brother shook his head at Edwin's sudden flourish.

Rose smiled as Edwin stood, and for the first time, she realized just how handsome his features really were.

"A pleasure to meet you both. I am Rose of Ametheria, and this is my companion, Joseph."

"Glad to make your acquaintance," Rauf said as they continued toward the palace. "Ametheria? We've had visitors from your land, but that was before my time. Are you staying or passing through?'

"I am uncertain of that yet," replied Rose.

"I would...*we* would be delighted if you stayed," Edwin said.

The group reached the steps leading up to the palace entrance. Many children ran and played on the stone steps, often weaving around four stationary guards who would smile as they passed. Upon seeing the quartet, and more importantly, the blonde horse and grey cat with them, several of the children bounded down the steps in excitement and ran over to touch and pet them. This delighted Rose, and she helped keep Wisher steady around the children's grasping hands. On the landing in front of the entrance, the children's mothers sat conversing. Among the ladies stood an elegantly dressed woman wearing a royal crown. She laughed with the others and spoke in a friendly manner. As the children made a commotion around Wisher and Snowflake, she glanced down, and her smile turned into a weary smirk, only mothers with sons possess, when she caught sight of Rauf and Edwin's haggard appearance.

"I suppose you're going to tell me this time you were trying to pull a whale from the river," the queen said as she descended the steps toward her children. "Or maybe fighting a pack of savage animals?"

Both boys looked downward, grinning. "Actually, there were these bandits..." Edwin began, and Rauf did his best to stifle a laugh.

"Enough," their mother said as she held up her hand. "Rauf Humphrey, get changed and go finish your work. Edwin

Cromwell, take those fish inside and have a bath drawn. Really, I sometimes wonder what I did to deserve...," The queen stopped as she spied Rose standing amongst the children.

Rose glanced upward and saw the queen staring at her with wide eyes and her mouth hanging open in silent, absolute shock. Joseph, Edwin, and Rauf stood looking from the queen to Rose and back again at the queen.

Rose finally broke the silence. "Your Highness? Is there something the matter?"

The queen descended the last steps and approached Rose. She stood facing her many moments before finally speaking.

"Isabel?" she asked in a whisper.

Now it was Rose's turn to be utterly taken aback. "Isabel is my mother's name. But how..."

The queen let out a delighted squeal that stopped everyone in earshot. She suddenly took Rose in her arms and hugged her tightly. "A daughter! A daughter!" she repeated. She then released Rose and looked her over. "Aside from the blonde hair, you look just like your mother! I thought I was seeing a ghost. How is she?"

"My Mother, the queen, is well, Your Highness," Rose said.

Now it was Edwin and Rauf's turn to stare in silence.

"*Queen* Isabel! Then, she completed her journey!"

Realization struck Rose, and suddenly, all became clear. "My mother's quest? She came here? You know of it?"

"Oh, yes, my dear, yes. Your mother and I were the best of friends during her short stay with us. Has she not spoke of me?"

"Take no offense, Your Highness," Rose assured. "It is forbidden to talk of the journey to the next heir who must take it."

"Oh, then, you and I have much to discuss. Your mother was a rambunctious one."

Rose delighted at the thought of hearing her mother's adventures, especially since "rambunctious" was not a word Rose associated with the woman that raised her. The queen gently shooed the surrounding children back to their mothers and motioned for a servant to take Wisher. Then, she and Rose walked up the palace steps and past a still silent Joseph, Edwin, and Rauf.

"How old are you, child?" the queen asked.

"Fifteen, Your Highness."

"A woman, now! Your mother was a couple of years older when she arrived. Oh, I've such fond memories of her. She taught me to play cards, you know? But where are my manners?" The queen stopped and curtseyed. "I am Queen Margaret Rose Engelbrecht, and I invite you to stay at my home, Princess..."

Rose curtseyed in return, "Princess Rose of Ametheria, Your Grace."

Another delighted squeal escaped from the queen. "Isabel named you after me?" she asked. The queen's giddiness was cut short as she took notice of Joseph for the first time. "Oh, forgive me. Are you one of Isabel's children, as well?"

Joseph bowed. "No, Your Highness, I am Joseph—Her Highness the Princess's traveling companion."

"Yes, of course. Isabel had a hand maiden journey with her." The queen leaned close to Rose. "Between you and me, she was more burden than help." The queen then turned back toward the palace and called one of her ladies of the court. "Please inform the staff that we have a royal guest staying with us, and have them prepare two rooms." The lady curtseyed and walked away.

"And you two," the queen said to her two boys, "go and make yourselves presentable as proper royal heirs. Hurry along now."

Rauf started up the stone steps, but Edwin paused and regarded Rose with a friendly grin. For a moment, Rose felt her heart beat a little faster as she looked at the prince before he turned and hurried away.

"We must make preparations!" Queen Margaret declared. "Come, we must get you to your rooms and to dinner. We've so many stories to tell each other."

"Yes, many stories," Rose said, distracted. She found it curious that she couldn't seem to take her thoughts off Prince Edwin. She turned to see where Joseph was and saw him holding Snowflake. Both he and the cat were staring at her with a wry look.

"What?" she asked.

Rose, Joseph, and Snowflake looked about the palace hall in amazement. The main hall served as a bustling commonwealth of people with markets and festive gatherings along both sides of the river flowing through it. Intricate carvings and colorful paintings were a delight to their eyes. The history of the village was told in a marvelous visual story that stretched the entire length of the cavernous room, which the queen delighted in translating for the newly arrived guests.

"So, your kingdom is completely self-sufficient?" Rose asked after the queen finished.

"Oh, yes," she said. "Thanks to the river ,we have cultivated surrounding land into farms, and we catch our fish in the town center, as you undoubtedly saw and smelled. And do you see how the river eventually flows through the opening at the other end of the hall? Beyond that, we have diverted channels from the river into great expanses of what are now wetlands--my great-great-grandfather's idea. And this hall itself was created from a natural cut in the cliff side made by the river. It serves exceptionally well for concerts and choirs in the evening, but we hold most celebrations in the ballroom upstairs from us."

"It is a magnificent achievement in craftsmanship, Your Highness," Rose said.

"Thank you, Princess."

"Your people do not travel outside the kingdom, then, Your Grace?" Joseph asked.

"We haven't seen the need to in generations. Occasionally, visitors such as yourselves discover us, and we do some trading. That's how we acquired the crops we grow in the wetlands. Oh, and my dear princess, you must remind me to tell you the story of a prank your mother helped me play on one of the local scoundrels who used to tease the ladies here. Your mother was a devilish trickster, if you do not mind me saying."

Rose's face lighted with the thoughts of her mother as a mischievous young lady. "I am most anxious to hear your stories, Your Highness."

"Your mother," the queen said softly. "I haven't thought about her in so long. I felt such a kinship to her, not in the least because we were both princesses set to rule our kingdoms one day. We spent a lot of time together talking about our impending rule. I think...I *know* we helped each other come to terms with some of the more frightening aspects of it. As wild as your mother was, and she was wild, she was also wise and thoughtful."

"She still is, Your Highness," Rose said. "Thank you for saying so."

Two servants approached the queen with a bow. "These two will show you to your rooms. I will send them back to inform you when dinner is prepared."

Rose curtseyed, and the servants led she and Joseph up a set of carved steps. One of the servants motioned for Joseph and led him down a separate hallway toward his quarters.

"See you at supper, then?" Joseph called out as he walked away.

"At supper." Rose felt uneasy for a moment as Joseph disappeared around a corner. The only time they had been quartered away from one another was during their cross over the ocean, and even then, their cabins had been next to each other. She allowed her uneasiness to dissipate as she followed the servant up the steps into a grand hallway. Instead of doors, heavy curtains hung in front of each room's entrance. The servant stopped in front of one of the curtains and pulled it aside with a bow. Rose curtseyed and stepped inside.

The bed chamber was as lavish as the rest of the palace. Rose was surprised to see hand-carved oaken bedroom furniture very much the same as what she had in her own chambers in Ametheria. She felt a quick pang of homesickness as she ran her hand along one of the bedposts.

A voice called through the curtain, asking permission to enter. After Rose granted it, a servant carrying Rose's belongings entered, followed by two handmaidens approximately Rose's age. "Good afternoon, Your Highness," one said. "We are to be your dressers for the evening. Do you require a bath drawn before the festivities tonight?"

"Festivities?" Rose asked.

"Oh, yes!" said the second handmaiden. She looked down for a moment in embarrassment but continued. "The Queen has called for a Barefoot Ball in your honor tonight. The first one this season."

"Barefoot Ball?"

"It's a long tradition in our kingdom," the first handmaiden said. "In times of great celebration, Her Highness holds a Barefoot Ball. All guests must remove their shoes and slippers before dancing on the ballroom floor."

"That sounds immensely fun," Rose said with a smile. "Where does this tradition come from?"

The second handmaiden beamed again in delight. "Why, from the legend of the golden slippers!" she said.

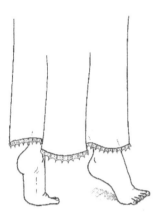

Chapter Fifteen

It was in the hallway just outside the ballroom where Rose reunited with Joseph for the first time since being escorted to their chambers; she had wondered if her friend would even recognize her. In place of the plain clothes she had worn was a flowing green gown with golden trim. Her face and hair were done to perfection, and she was truly the image of her mother, in all her beauty and radiance. She walked among the people, waiting for the ballroom to open. She chatted pleasantly with each person who greeted her but smiled brightest when she caught sight of Joseph.

"You, dear sir, would make an excellent addition to my court in those clothes," she said with a curtsey.

Joseph bowed. "My dear princess, it is my displeasure to decline your royal invitation, for the itching of these garments would be madness to me," he said in an arrogant yet silly voice, his nose turned up.

Rose laughed and hugged Joseph. He extended an arm, Rose took it with a nod, and they walked among the crowd. "I had almost forgotten what it was like to wear a gown again," Rose said. "Though their fashion of gowns is more comfortable than my mother's; very hard to breathe in corsets."

"I would imagine, especially in the curves you now possess."

Rose cried out in embarrassed shock and slapped Joseph on the shoulder. "Really!"

"I humbly beg your apologies, Princess, but you must admit your...*shape* does suit your garment. You will be an appealing sight to the other guests—especially to a certain prince, perhaps?"

Rose eyed Joseph with a smirk. "Perhaps. Prince Edwin does seem to have taken a fancy to me."

"Indeed," replied Joseph, not returning her gaze. "He made that understood from the conversation we had."

Rose stopped and turned Joseph to face her. "And what conversation was this?"

"Oh, he came to my chamber to inquire about you. About us. Were we to be married and such?" Joseph laughed at Rose's sudden look of disgust. "My thoughts exactly."

"So, he is smitten?"

"That is too mild a word for what he is." Joseph took Rose again by the arm and they continued walking. "And, if I may be so bold, what are your feelings toward the prince?"

"What would you have me say? I met him mere hours ago."

Just then, several young pages stepped through the large curtains covering the various entrances to the ballroom. In unison, they parted the curtains and stood silently as the guests began to file in.

"I say, let us enjoy ourselves tonight," Joseph said as he led Rose into the ballroom.

For the rest of her days, whenever Rose thought about the inventiveness or artistry of man, her mind would always first recall the room in which she currently stood. It was an enormous chamber inside the heart of the palace that reached high above to a domed ceiling. The dome, cut and polished, reflected the colors of the earth back from the torchlight shining upon it. This gave the entire chamber a warm glow that changed hue as a person moved through it. Tables and seating carved from the stone earth occupied the surrounding floor of the ballroom for dining; the dance floor in the center as smooth as water in a pond on a still, summer day. Beyond that, the dais for the royal family and court stood where Queen Margaret sat and chatted with her husband, King Gregory. The king was pleasant-looking with a bushy beard and even bushier hair spilling from his crown. When Queen Margaret spied Rose and Joseph, she rose to her feet, smiling, and beckoned them over. As they approached, Rose noticed that Prince Edwin was not present with the rest of the family, and, in realizing she had noticed in the first place, silently scolded herself.

"Your Majesties," Joseph announced with a bow, "may I present Her Royal Highness Princess Rose of Ametheria."

Rose curtseyed. The king rose and bowed, and the queen curtseyed in return. "We are honored to have such a distinguished guest with us tonight," Queen Margaret said. "Please be seated and be well."

"And forgive our missing son, Edwin," the king said with a bit of irritation. "The boy isn't what you would call timely.... Well, there's the little whelp now."

Edwin appeared from behind a curtain, one hand dropping from his breast where he had been adjusting a button on his jacket. He looked at Rose and seemed to go into a silent panic, but he quickly composed himself and strode confidently over to the princess. He took her hand with a bow and kissed it.

"My apologies for being late, Your Highness," he said.

"You should be sorry, boy," the king said. "And is that yet another jacket you have on? What was the matter with the other four?"

Prince Rauf, standing next to his mother, stifled a laugh as Queen Margaret gave the king a slight nudge. Looking embarrassed, Edwin managed to ask Rose if he may escort her to her seat. She smiled, nodded, and took the prince's arm in hers as they mounted the dais.

Joseph turned and faced the king and queen. "If it pleases the court, I shall take my leave and talk with your subjects before we dine." The royals gave Joseph a slight nod as he made one final bow and walked into the crowd as Rose took her seat next to the queen.

"Your Highness," Rose said to Queen Margaret, "excuse my boldness, but I'd like to inquire about some of the mischievous pranks my mother seemed so fond in making in her youth."

Queen Margaret smiled, a youthful twinkle in her eyes and a near-wicked turn in her lips and Rose knew she was in for some surprising stories.

The supper was wonderful, and the conversation even more so, in Rose's opinion. Queen Margaret's stories of Princess Isabel's time in her land, some of which would have surely embarrassed her mother, were some of the most humorous tales Rose had ever heard and she swore on each one that she would not breathe a word about it back home. As she and the queen spoke, Rose would catch small glimpses from Prince Edwin, which would cause him to quickly become preoccupied with something else. If Queen Margaret took any notice of these affectionate glances, she made no sign of it, but Rose could not help but believe a mother knew her son's heart. Other times, Rose would spy Joseph mingling with the guests, particularly with the maidens. She chuckled as he gestured and performed for the ladies, obviously regaling them with tales of their adventures. At one point, he thrilled five maidens by reenacting his fight with Captain Gold Tooth with so much flourish, Rose could not look at him any longer for fear of bursting out in full laughter.

A ringing echoed in the ballroom. The queen stood holding brass chimes, which she hit with a small mallet. The room grew quiet after a few moments, and all eyes turned to her.

"My most loyal subjects," she began, "tonight we celebrate the arrival of a very special guest to our kingdom--a guest of great importance to me, Her Highness, Princess Rose of Ametheria."

Rose stood to the sound of great applause. She marveled at how the ballroom amplified and carried the sound evenly over the entire space. She curtseyed and seated herself again.

"Princess Rose is the eldest daughter of Queen Isabel of Ametheria, a dear friend from my youth. I fear I've been taking up much of our evening with telling stories of her mother to Her

Highness, so we will commence now with our tradition of the Barefoot Ball."

"Your Highness?" asked Rose. "I have heard that the tradition of the Barefoot Ball is rooted in a legend of golden slippers. If I may, could you tell us strangers to your land—me and my traveling companion Joseph—of this legend before we commence?"

"Why, I would be delighted, Princess," the queen said as, from behind her, the king rolled his eyes. As everyone in the palace sat, the queen stepped to the front of the dais and began to speak.

"Long ago, when the Great Palace of the Kingdom Engelbrecht was cut from the canyon walls, there was a princess named Caroline. Princess Caroline was the spirit of joy, and that joy took many forms, but the most well-known was that of dance. She danced so much, she wore out her dancing slippers every single day, which annoyed her father, King William. The king found dancing, in general, to be silly and a waste of time. He considered it a point of pride that he had never danced one step in his entire life. At times, the king wished his daughter would stop her foolishness and never dance again.

"As the princess grew, so did her fondness for dancing, and she began to wear out multiple pairs of slippers daily. King William knew something must be done, so he sent his most trusted knight on a quest to find someone who could make a pair of slippers that would never wear out. After a three-year quest, the knight returned with a most unusual being: an elfish tailor. The tailor vowed to create a pair of slippers that would never wear away, and, in a matter of days, he presented the slippers to the king.

"Never had any person laid eyes on such a magnificent pair of slippers, spun from the finest gold and glimmered as if from their own light. The tailor told the king the slippers were enchanted and they would only be worn by the royal feet that needed them.

"At first, the princess was overjoyed at her present, and at the following royal ball, the princess put the slippers on for the first time and began to dance in the middle of the ballroom floor.

"But something was wrong. As the slippers danced along the ground, they grew heavier and heavier with each step. They grew so heavy, they left scratches in the stone floor of the ballroom. After many minutes, the princess ceased dancing. The king's heart broke in two at the sight of his daughter, joyless, standing motionless in the middle of the dance floor. Slowly, the princess removed the slippers from her feet and stood barefoot, weeping.

"Suddenly, the king called to his daughter. She turned to see her father remove his shoes and stockings. He approached her, took her hands in his and the two danced. The daughter was overjoyed and danced freer than she ever had. It was when the dance was over that the princess and king noticed the golden slippers had disappeared, but to a father and daughter, closer than they had ever been before, it was not important, soon forgotten in the joy of that night's festivities.

"That was the first Barefoot Ball," said the queen, "and tonight, we honor our guest with our tradition. May she dance as free as Princess Caroline did so many ages ago."

Princess Rose stood and curtseyed to the kingdom as they applauded. "Your Grace, with permission, may your son Edwin join me in my first dance?"

Before the queen could reply, Prince Edwin was on his feet and in front of Rose. He took her hand and bowed. "I would be most delighted," he said, escorting her from the dais to the center of the dance floor.

Edwin and Rose bowed to each other and removed their shoes, retrieved immediately by a servant. They stepped forward and held hands as Edwin slipped one arm around her side. The music began, and the two glided around the floor.

"You are wonderful," the prince said.

"You are being too kind, Your Highness. My mother, the queen, always provided us with the best instructors but dance has never been my greatest talent...."

"I wasn't talking about your dancing."

Rose looked into Edwin's eyes and saw they were sincere. They continued dancing as the rest of the kingdom's subjects joined them on the floor, and they continued dancing for much of the ball.

As the third hour of celebration began, many of the kingdom's subjects, who were still in attendance, sat and chatted casually. Joseph and King George talked by the dais, and the queen was entertaining her court of ladies, while Rauf entertained some ladies of his own. Rose and Edwin had just begun another dance together when, without warning, Rose stopped.

"What is that?" she asked, looking downward.

"What?" Edwin replied.

Rose ran her foot over the smooth, stone surface of the dance floor. "Do you feel that?"

Edwin ran his foot over the same spot. "I feel...nothing. What am I feeling for?"

"A cut or groove in the floor. I have felt it several times while dancing tonight. Have you not noticed it?"

"Your Highness, forgive me, but I have danced on this floor most of my life, and I've never felt any grooves. It's as smooth as a looking glass."

Rose didn't reply. She concentrated on the way the floor felt under her. Slowly, she traced the groove with her toe until it stopped. As she did so, she felt another groove under her other foot and traced it, as well. Edwin stood back, looking as Rose steadily moved across the dance floor, sliding her feet without lifting them from the ground.

"It feels...familiar. A pattern of sorts," Rose said, more to herself than Edwin. She continued to slide her foot across the floor as others began to take note of the princess's strange behavior. It felt, to her, as if she were performing a slow, careful...

"Dance!" Rose cried out. "The grooves form a pattern of two feet performing a dance. Do you see?" All eyes were on Rose as she looked at the prince, delighted in her discovery. Edwin stood mute and Rose huffed in irritation.

"Look, here," she said as she walked over to a seemingly random place on the floor. "It starts right here where I am standing. Let me see if I can follow it." Rose moved her feet across the floor, her eyes closed and concentrating on the feeling beneath her. Everyone in the hall watched as the princess danced as if in a trance. She moved with more confidence as the pattern became more familiar to her. After a minute, she twirled and came to rest. The pattern had ended.

A loud clattering from the direction of the royal dais caused Rose's eyes to jolt open. The queen stood, a goblet she had been holding was now at her feet, once again her eyes wide and mouth open in surprise in Rose's direction.

Slowly, Rose looked around. Every person stared at her with the same look of disbelief. Rose looked at Edwin, ready to apologize for whatever insult she made, but stopped. Edwin bore the same look of surprise, but, being the closest to Rose, she saw that he was looking in her direction but not at her. Rather, the prince's gaze transfixed on something on the floor in front of her. Rose looked downward but knew what she would see before she saw them.

On the ground, a short distance in front of her, as if they had been there the entire time, were the golden slippers.

Rose grinned at the sight of the shining slippers facing her. She looked at Queen Margaret, who smiled, clasping her hands in joy. She looked at Rose, silently nodded and motioned for her to take the slippers. Rose nodded in reply and took a step forward.

The slippers took a step back.

A loud, surprised gasp from the crowd echoed through the room. Rose blinked her eyes, unsure of what she had just witnessed. She took another step forward, and the slippers took another one back. Rose paused and slowly moved one foot forward. The matching slipper slowly moved backward. Rose took a step back. One slipper stepped forward. Rose moved one foot upward in front of her allowing it to hang in the air. One slipper moved back, and, as if worn on an invisible leg, hung in the air, as well. Rose waited a moment, then suddenly, dashed forward reaching for the slippers. The slippers just as rapidly dashed backward away from her grasp. Rose stopped. The slippers stopped. Rose took a breath, then leaped in the air to fall on top of them, but the slippers moved away, allowing Rose to sprawl across the ground. Rose looked up and fumed at the sight of the slippers, one of which tapped its toe at her.

Rose pulled herself up from the humiliating position on the floor. She stared at the slippers in a silent, burning frustration. She moved forward but halted. As the slippers continued tapping, Rose let her irritation fade, and she focused on the sound of the gold toe ticking against the stone floor. Slowly, Rose heard something in the tapping: a rhythm. She tapped her bare toe on the ground in the same manner as the slipper. The slippers seemed to respond in kind by the heels bouncing ever so slightly. Rose followed suit and felt as if she could hear a tune; not with her ears, but her whole body. She watched the slippers and saw them spring to life in a dance. Quickly, she matched the slippers' steps and found herself dancing in a manner she had never seen or been taught before. Unlike the rigid pattern of steps she had been instructed for years, Rose discovered, to her delight, this free form of dancing came naturally to her. Tapping her feet on the floor, she bounced and swirled across the floor in an energetic pace. Had the slippers faces, they would have grinned, for they danced joyously.

The entire kingdom watched the lively spectacle. Rose stopped matching the exact movement of the slippers, and instead, danced in a complimentary way to her enchanted partner. Clapping began. Others cheered. Some danced among the seats. The queen gestured to the royal musicians, and in seconds, they played a boisterous tune in rhythm with the dancing slippers.

Rose hardly noticed all the commotion around her. She danced with the slippers as flawlessly as if they were a part of her own being. She laughed as the slippers performed a breezy, spirited shuffle. She did so, as well, marveling at the human body's ability to perform such motions. The slippers did a little hop in her direction, and she did one toward them. As the dance reached a peak, Rose and the slippers did one magnificent leap in the air. The slippers landed on the floor, and Rose's feet landed neatly in them. They fit her feet perfectly.

Cheers and applause exploded through the great hall. Rose burst out in overjoyed laughter and looked over at Joseph. Her friend simply smirked at her and nodded his head, indication he was not surprised at all in her ability to do practically anything.

Chapter Sixteen

The Queen expressed much dismay, early the next morning, when Rose announced their departure. Many plans were made for more festivities, but Rose refused any fuss over leaving. Rose placed the golden slippers in a bundle containing the other pieces of her coronation gown. After breakfast, Joseph went off with Snowflake to prepare Wisher for the last leg of the journey as Rose said her goodbyes to the royal family.

"Your mother will be so proud of you," Queen Margaret said as she embraced Rose. "My family and I are all impressed with the lady you are."

"Some of us a little more than impressed, perhaps?" Rauf said to Edwin, teasing him. But Edwin did not seem to be in any mood for jokes or teases. He stood soberly with his family as the king approached Rose.

"For all I know of your mother, you have a lot to live up to, young lady," he said. "And, from what I've seen last night, you should have no problems with that."

"Thank you, Your Highness."

Rauf stepped forward and bowed. "You truly have given our kingdom a night that shall be discussed for generations, Princess. Our many thanks."

Rose nodded, and Edwin stepped forward. He took her hand in his, kissed it, and bowed. "May our paths cross again soon, Your Highness."

"I would like that," she said as she curtseyed. Rose then turned and joined Joseph. She mounted Wisher and, after Joseph swung himself up to the rear of the saddle, waved goodbye as they left the palace steps and began their trek back through the canyon.

Rose remained quiet for most of the journey, speaking only of slight pleasantries when they occurred to her. Joseph never pursued any topic concerning Prince Edwin until the afternoon of the day they exited the canyon.

"I believe I shall miss that place," Joseph said looking back down the canyon to the river and green surrounding it.

"Yes," replied Rose. "Even after witnessing the majesty of the mermaid kingdom, I believe the kingdom of Engelbrecht will always be the foremost in my mind."

"Prince Edwin seemed to take quite a liking to you."

"The prince, if you must know, was an absolute gentleman," Rose stated. "His feelings toward me were not unnoticed, but I do have other pressing concerns than a blossoming romance, do I not?"

For a moment, Rose was silent, "However, it was refreshing having my thoughts on something other than this quest. We have been on it so long that I have often felt lost to it; that it is all that I am anymore."

Joseph looked at the princess as she spoke, his brows furrowed in worry.

Sensing this, Rose turned her head back toward Joseph and gave him a half-smile. "Being a queen always seemed like a natural part of who I was going to become. When we began this journey, I realized it was something that I needed to earn. But in earning, I felt like I left myself behind—the girl who rode horses, played with swords, and teased her sisters. I quietly have been resenting the quest. Hating it at times. But after speaking with Queen Margaret about her time spent with Mother, her kingdom and family..." The princess sat on her steed, gathering her thoughts and finding words to convey her spectrum of emotions. "Through her, I see the joy in being grown up. And I now know I am ready to be Queen."

"You have been ready since the day I met you, Princess," Snowflake said from the comfort of her lap. "You may not have known it, but you were. This journey is a formality written in spells and magic I can't begin to comprehend, but still only a formality. In my opinion, at least."

"And I have seen the child grow to womanhood," Joseph said. "Not because you turned a certain age, but because of your wisdom, intellect, and compassion that only a ruler possesses."

Joseph reached around Rose and pulled on Wisher's reins bringing the horse to a stop. She turned in the saddle and saw a look of unquestionable sincerity in the face of her friend.

"It will be my proudest day when I can bow before you as my queen," he said.

Rose struggled for a response, but before she could speak, a soft clattering sounded from the bundle containing her golden gown. After a moment, she and Joseph could see movement from inside it. Rose quickly dismounted and untied the bundle from Wisher's back. She opened the bundle and removed the golden slippers. She examined them carefully until a moment of inspiration struck her. She knelt and placed the slippers on the desert floor. The slippers turned slightly on their heels and walked at a brisk pace.

"Where are they going?" Joseph asked.

Rose mounted the horse and grinned.

"To the golden crown."

Chapter Seventeen

Through many lands and many weeks, the slippers walked. Some lands were lush and full of life, others were desolate but containing their own beauty. These days would be filled with laughter, meeting new friends, enjoying new experiences, and an occasional adventure. Passing through one village, Rose bartered for a parchment scroll, pen, and ink. It was during this period, she recorded her memories and thoughts of the journey, which she hoped would make for good bedtime reading for her youngest sister, though it did occur to the princess that Violet may be too grown for bedtime stories when Rose returned home. At nights, she would write, and during the days, she read her writings aloud to Joseph and Snowflake, who would add details Rose had not witnessed and marvel at the ones they had forgotten, but Rose remembered. Joseph visibly winced as Rose read of her harrowing struggles in the bowels of Captain Gold Tooth's ship. Had the pirate who struck her been in their company as she read it, Rose felt that Joseph would have perhaps slain the fiend then and there. This final leg of their travels was the most pleasant for all, perhaps because they could feel the journey drawing closer to an end.

It would be the day before Rose's sixteenth birthday that the slippers stopped for all time. Rose and her companions found themselves at the bottom of a grassy valley surrounded by rolling, green hills. Had Rose not known any better, she would have sworn she had somehow returned to her homeland. In the distance stood two structures unlike any Rose had ever seen. The first was a lone, thin tower of white stone stretching into the sky, higher that any she had ever seen before. It seemed to almost touch the clouds. While she could make out an opening and balcony on top, she could not see any door or entrance at the base. The other structure was an puzzle as to its purpose or even its shape. It appeared to be made of solid metal, perhaps tarnished bronze. If Rose judged correctly from their distance, it was fifteen meters in height and stretched nearly a hundred meters in length. At first glance, the sides were smooth, but upon further inspection, she discovered some indentions and curves in the side of the structure.

Rose dismounted and picked the slippers from the grass. "Thank you," she whispered to them as she placed them back in the clothes bundle.

It was another hour crossing the valley floor before they arrived at the base of the tower. As Joseph examined the metal structure, Rose walked around the tower, searching for an opening. Before long, Rose came across what appeared to be a stoned-up doorway. The doorway was comprised of an arch of blocks with a diamond-shaped rock at its upper point. The stones that filled the doorway blocking any entrance seemed to consist of the same ones the tower itself was created from. Rose pushed on the stone wall within the doorway and found it to be as solid as the tower.

"Joseph!" Rose called out, and within moments, her companion stood next to her, examining the doorway. Together, Rose and Joseph pushed against the barrier. After many minutes of struggle, they declared their efforts hopeless. They then turned to examining the doorway, carefully looking for any crack or seam that might help them gain entry.

"Maybe we can dig underneath?" Joseph suggested.

Agreeing it was worth a try, Rose and Joseph knelt and pushed aside the grass from the base of the rock barrier. To their dismay, they found that the barrier extended well into the earth, but their next discovery caused them to forget their disappointment.

Into one of the larger stones in the base of the rock wall, a series of words had been chiseled. Rose read aloud:

The final piece awaits within.
One key of rock.
Another key for the lock.
Only the perceptive will gain perspective.

Rose and Joseph looked at each other.

"I will set up camp," Joseph sighed. "We are due to be here for a while, I would imagine."

As Rose, Joseph and Snowflake ate their supper, they discussed the possible meanings of the riddle in the stone. All agreed each line of the riddle held a clue. The first was obvious: the crown awaited Rose in the tower, likely at the top. The second and third revealed that two keys were needed to obtain the crown. The final line of the riddle, however, proved to be a mystery to them all. They discussed it well into the night until finally bedding down. As he had done almost every night since joining them on the journey, Snowflake eventually wandered over to Rose and crawled under her blanket, curling up against her stomach. Rose petted the cat as she lay there, looking toward the tower and, quite possibly, her destiny within.

The next morning, Rose, Joseph, and Snowflake decided to examine the odd metal structure before returning to ponder the riddle in the stone. They paced around the object once to determine its shape. For the most part, it was a long, smooth-surfaced, thin rectangle with two extensions on one end that did not seem to serve any purpose. The other end of the object curved around in almost a complete circle before joining the rectangle part. For a couple of hours, the three circled the metal thing but could find no means of either entering or opening it. At one point, Rose and Joseph tried to lift Snowflake on top of the structure but could not, even when standing upon Wisher's saddle. Finally, they decided to rest and return to trying to solve the riddle.

Rose, Joseph, and Snowflake sat in a circle as Rose took out her scroll and wrote out the riddle. "'One key of rock.' Let us discuss that," she said. "That must mean something more than we are thinking."

"You mean, besides a key that is made from a rock," Snowflake replied.

"Yes. I think it is misleading. When you read it, you think of a key that has been chiseled from stone."

"That is what I assume," Joseph interjected. "But that is impractical. Even the hardest of stone cut as thin as a key would break in any lock you would turn it in."

"And the riddle mentions a lock," Snowflake said.

"Yes, but the lock mentioned is for a different key," Rose said. "What if the key of stone is not used in a lock?"

"Why would you make that conclusion?" Joseph asked.

"Because the riddle is specific. Look. The second line says, 'One key of rock.' The third, 'Another key for the lock.' The second line makes no mention of any lock, while the third does. It is our assumption that the first key is for a lock. As well, the third line refers to 'the' lock which sounds as if there is only one."

"It appears your years of language lessons have borne fruit," Joseph said.

"Yes, but a key without a lock is rather pointless, is it not?" Snowflake asked.

"That is because we are thinking of a *normal* key," Rose replied. "What other kinds of keys are there besides lock keys?"

"I am afraid you have me there," the cat replied.

"I think the real clue in the line is the word 'rock,'" Joseph said. "What kind of key is a rock?"

"A 'rock key?'" Snowflake asked.

"'Stone key?'" Rose pondered.

There was a moment of silence before Joseph sat upright. "Hold on a moment. Say that again, Rose."

"'Stone key.'"

"Now switch the words."

"Key st..." Her eyes grew wide, and she and Joseph leaped to their feet and dashed toward the tower.

"Hey, now!" Snowflake shouted as he hurried along behind them. "That is not sporting, leaving me out of it!"

The trio stopped in front of the blocked archway and looked up at the diamond-shaped rock in the middle. "A keystone," Rose said. She reached up and tried to grasp the rock, wedging her fingernails in the seams between it and the surrounding stones. She pulled as hard as she could, but the rock showed no give. She then tried pushing against it, but it still held fast. She finally dropped her arms in frustration.

"I know this is the answer," she said. "I know it."

Everyone remained silent as the princess stared at the keystone. Even the forest itself seemed to grow quiet as Rose thought. Finally, she turned to Joseph. "That stone is the key to entering the door, correct?"

"I would believe so."

"And how do you use a door key?"

Joseph smiled. "You turn it."

Rose reached up, grasped the keystone on both sides and turned it. The rock rotated without the slightest resistance; the surrounding arch stones swiveling as it moved. Suddenly, as Rose twisted the keystone sideways, the arch and the rocks within began to collapse on themselves like a house of cards. Rose backed away as the barrier continued to fall, cracking against each other and landing on the ground with soft thumps. In seconds, where a blocked doorway once stood, was now a dark opening. Cautiously, Rose approached the opening and leaned inside. She could see sunlight streaming in from multiple, tiny gaps in between the rocks that comprised the tower, and in the dim glow of that sunlight was a rickety staircase winding upward.

Joseph stepped forward, but Rose turned and placed a gentle hand on his chest, halting him. "Best you do not look, Joseph," she said with a nervous smile, "or you might try and convince me not to go." Rose took one more glance back in the tower and the staircase. "What is more, you might succeed."

"We both know by now, I cannot talk you out of anything, Rose," Joseph said. Just then, he turned away and walked back to their camp. Rose saw him kneel and open one of their bundles. After a few moments, he returned to her. Draped in his arms was her golden gown. When he spoke, there was a quiver in his voice that made Rose's heart break.

"I do not know why, but something is telling me it is time," he said, and slowly held out the gown to Rose.

The princess stood for a moment, looking down at the gold material shining up at her. She reached over and glided one hand across the intricate weaving. She looked back up at the face of her traveling companion and lifelong friend. "You have given up so much for me, Joseph. Thank you."

"I have gained more than I have given, I think."

"But these years alone with only me as your companion. Others might be married by your age, and fathers by the time we return home."

"And I have seen sights no commoner would ever hope to see, lived adventures one would only hear about in bedtime stories, and all in the company of my truest friend. I have no regrets, Your Highness."

No more words would be spoken. Rose took the gown from Joseph's arms. Joseph picked up Snowflake, gave him a scratch behind the ears, and walked around the tower and out of sight.

Rose took a breath. The doorway of the tower was dark but, in it, she saw the end of a journey spanning three years. She stepped in. In the dim light, Rose removed her outer garments. Piece by piece, she put on the gown. The weight of the gold seemed to disappear as she clothed herself in it. Finally, Rose placed her feet in the slippers. Everything fit perfectly.

Standing straight, she walked out into the sunlight. The gown felt warm, comforting. She rounded the tower and stood on the small rise, looking down at her beloved friends.

Snowflake was the first to see her. Joseph seemed to notice the cat's stare and he turned. They both looked at the majestic woman before them. Joseph took Snowflake in his arms and rose to his feet. He placed the cat on Wisher's back and, taking the reins, led them up the hill, stopping in front of Rose. She patted Wisher on the nose in a silent thanks for carrying her. She then scratched Snowflake's ears, grinning at his pleasant purring. She then turned toward Joseph. Words could not express the gratitude she felt toward him. She held out her hand for his. Joseph looked down at but didn't take it. Instead, he bent down and kneeled in front of his friend and future queen. Rose stifled a sob in her throat and her heart ached for a time now behind them. She placed her outstretched hand gently on his bowed head. When she removed it, Joseph turned his head upward.

But she was already gone.

Rose stood inside the tower looking up at the staircase. She thought of each year of her journey and each new friend she had encountered, and she was surprised at her sadness of it all reaching its final moments. Carefully, she placed one foot on the first step. The staircase groaned, seemingly in the pain of old age. Rose started upward. Time seemed to slow as Rose climbed higher and higher up the tower. She ignored the ache in her legs, the dull, pulsing pain in her feet, as she continued. She thought of Wisher, Joseph, and Snowflake. She thought of Queen Margaret and Prince Edwin. She thought of her sisters and her father. She thought of her mother. And, finally, Rose reached the top of the staircase. It ended at a wooden floor with a trap door cut into it. Rose placed her hands against the door and, crying out slightly from the pressure on her legs, pushed the heavy door upward.

The door swung open and fell to the floor with a startling bang. Rose spilled out of the opening onto the floor but managed to stop her fall. She sat on the floor and closed her eyes against the sudden cramping pain shooting up from her legs. There, she stayed until the pain eased away. She opened her eyes, and immediately, she saw a light streaming in from the balcony opening. She stood, painfully, to walk over to it but stopped when she realized there was a glow emanating from behind her. She turned toward the center of the room. Hanging in the air, as if on an invisible pedestal, was a crystal box with a brass lock. Inside the box was the golden crown.

The crown itself was surprisingly ordinary without a single jewel adorning it. The gold surface was flawlessly smooth. The front of the crown was slightly raised to a curved point, and engraved in it was the crest of Ametheria.

As Rose looked at the crown, all the weariness and pain from her grueling climb up the tower faded away. She placed her hands on top of the crystal box and was not surprised by its soothing warmth. After a moment, she turned and walked out onto the balcony. She leaned over to call down to her friends to let them know she had made it safely to the top, when she stopped. From her perch, high above in the tower, Rose saw the mysterious metal structure in the valley floor below fully for the first time.

It was in the shape of a large key.

As the sun began to set, Rose found herself still considering the puzzle before her. It had been hours since she had spied the large key below, but she had no answer as to how a key so enormous could open the tiny lock on the crystal box. She had vainly searched the tower chamber many times over for anything that might prove to be a clue. Once, she even tried to take the crystal box down the tower, but she was unable to budge it from its position in the air. Rose knew she was one step away from ending her journey, but what was that step?

She walked back out onto the balcony and looked at the sun, sinking to the horizon. She knew if she didn't come up with the answer soon, she would have to walk back down the tower stairs and return the following morning. The steps would be too dangerous to walk on in darkness and, as the air began to chill, Rose knew she could not stay in the chamber through the night.

For the countless time, Rose looked back down at the key. Her friends were almost too small for her to make out, but the key was large enough and plain to see. From the height Rose stood, it practically looked the right size to fit...

Only the perceptive will gain perspective.

...the lock.

And she had the answer.

Slowly, deliberately, Rose reached her hand downward toward the key below. She placed her hand between her view and the key until her hand blocked all sight of it. She then closed her fingers into a fist. She gasped as she felt her hand clutching something. She pulled her hand back, turned it over, and opened her fingers. The key was in her palm. In the earth far below, all that was left was the sunken impression where the key once rested.

Rose walked to the crystal box and inserted the key in the lock. The latch inside clicked as she turned the key. The lid to the crystal box slowly swung open, and the crown floated up and out of its beautiful prison. It hung in the air in front of Rose's eyes. Holding her breath in eagerness, Rose reached out with both hands and grasped the crown. She brought it closer to her and looked down at it with a smile.

A sudden tremor ripped through the tower and threw Rose from the floor into the air. She crashed down on her back and let out a cry of pain and terror. Another shockwave bounced her across the room before she could regain her senses. Somewhere in the rumbling noise filling the chamber, she could hear the crown clattering across the room. Rose clutched the wall and pulled herself to her feet as the shaking of the tower grew stronger. To her horror, she could see the stones in the walls shaking loose. Ground up rock dust filled the chamber, choking her. Stumbling, she made her way to the balcony to fill her lungs with fresh air. Poking her head out of the opening, but not daring to step onto the balcony itself for fear of it coming apart under her, she took deep, gaping breaths. But when she looked out at the landscape surrounding the tower, her breath caught in her chest as she stared in numbing disbelief.

The valley surrounding the tower crumbled and began to disappear. No, not disappear; it was violently ripped apart by an unseen force. The trees splintered and soared into the air. The surrounding hills exploded in a wave of earth and flew upward. Rose looked to the sky, and her mind reeled from what she saw.

A vortex hung in the air as if the sky itself had been torn open. Trees, rocks, and debris tumbled into it. Rose tore her horrified eyes away from it just as the balcony ripped from the side of the tower. Rose looked down at the remaining ground below. She could see no sign of her friends.

As if a giant had kicked the side of the tower, the entire structure suddenly lurched, and Rose found herself thrown upward and outward into the air. She thrust a hand out and grasped the few remaining boards from the balcony. The wind whipped at her as she struggled to pull herself back up to the opening.

As her head began to crest over the bottom of the opening, she heard the clattering of the crown and saw it rapidly bouncing toward her. She reached with one hand in a desperate effort to grab it, when the crown struck a board that had broken upward from the floor. It bounced just out of Rose's reach as it sailed out and down into open space.

Without thinking, Rose thrust one leg outward, and the crown caught on the toe of her slipper. Rose took a deep breath, and with strength she didn't believe she contained any longer, she pulled herself cautiously, steadily back into the chamber.

Rose fell to the floor as the tremors continued. She could now hear the rocks in the walls of the tower below her coming apart and ripping away. The shingles of the ceiling tore from above flying into the hole in the sky. The world seemed to be coming apart in great, violent waves.

And in this destruction, Princess Rose stood up, holding the crown. She never let her eyes waver from it and her reflection looking back at her. And in her mind, she could hear the voice of her mother. And her father. And her sisters.

Time to come home.

Rose closed her eyes and placed the crown on her head.

Then, there was silence.

Chapter Eighteen

Rose opened her eyes. The world around her seemed to be flooded in a bright, blurry haze. A breeze gently brushed against her, and she could hear songbirds in the distance. As her eyes focused, Rose looked down and saw her feet planted firmly on cobblestone. The golden gown looked none the worse for wear from the destruction she had been standing in moments ago.

"Rose?"

The princess looked up at the familiar voice. Just a few feet away, stood Joseph, Wisher, and Snowflake. Just as Rose was, none of them looked as if they had been in the center of the ground-shattering chaos that had surrounded them. The expression in their eyes, even Wisher's, reflected her own confusion.

"Are we well?" Joseph asked. "The last thing I remember the world seemed to be going mad."

Rose did not answer. Even in her joy at seeing her friends unharmed and by her side, she began to notice their surroundings—their very familiar surroundings. She looked at the spacious cobblestone floor they stood on, where many a festive banquet held, at the neighboring courtyard field where she enjoyed many hours riding upon her beloved Wisher, at the stables where Joseph spent his childhood caring for the royal horses, and finally, at the grand palace behind her.

She was home.

Rose let out a joyous laugh. She ran over to her friends, scooping up Snowflake and whirling around. She danced over to Wisher and placed Snowflake on his back. She happily stroked Wisher's forehead, who nuzzled softly against her chest. Finally, she turned to Joseph. The two friends exchanged a silent look; a thank you. And completely unnoticed by the quartet, the people of the palace—servants, guards, guests—trickled out into the courtyard as word of the remarkable strangers began to circulate.

Hurried footsteps echoed outward from one of the halls. Rose turned to see her mother run from the doorway, her gown hiked up almost to her knees as she sprinted. The queen stopped short upon seeing the statuesque woman, who was once the young lady she had last seen many years ago. Neither mother nor daughter spoke as they raced to each other in the middle of the courtyard and embraced to the cheers and applause of the surrounding crowd. Though Rose was now no longer the child she had been, the comfort of her mother's arms felt the same as when she was little.

Queen Isabel released Rose and stepped back, tears glistening on her face. "Was it appropriate for a mother to hug her daughter, the queen, or should I have curtseyed?"

"A mother always hugs her daughter, especially one who loves her so." The two women hugged again as the hearty, joyous voice of Rose's father resounded over the cheering.

"My daughter!" the king said as he exited the palace and saw Rose with her mother. His other four daughters immediately followed, who called out their sister's name as they all ran to her. Rose wrapped her arms around her father as he kissed her on the cheek. Her sisters surrounded her and held her in turn, all speaking at once, and all saying how much she had changed. Rose, likewise, noticed, with a little sadness, how much her sisters had grown up without her. The princesses all marveled at her golden gown and begged to be told of Rose's adventures.

"Cease!" King Charles commanded. "There shall be no more discussion until a grand banquet is assembled. Page! Page!" A young lad Rose did not recognize approached the king. "To the kitchens, and tell the cooks to begin preparations for tonight. I want nothing less than their culinary masterpieces! Then spread the word throughout the kingdom that the Prin...that their *new queen* has arrived!"

The page bowed and was off in a hurry.

"So many changes," Rose remarked.

"Oh, that is Reginald," said the youngest sister, Violet.

"Violet *liiiikes* Reg-in-ald," Daisy taunted.

Violet gave Daisy a kick.

"And some things do not change," Rose followed. The entire family laughed as they walked toward the hallway entrance. Rose stopped and looked back. Joseph had turned away and was leading Wisher to the stables.

"A moment, please," she told her family and hurried over to her friend. "Joseph."

Joseph turned.

"Your queen requests…" Rose hesitated and shook her head at the sound of the words. "I would like my friend to be a guest of honor at tonight's banquet."

Joseph smiled. "You wish this just so I have to dress in frilly clothing again, are you not?" They both chuckled and he bowed. "It is *my* honor, Your Highness."

Rose turned and rejoined her family. Her sisters excitedly peppered her with questions as they all entered the palace.

Even with few hours to prepare, all who attended that night's banquet in Rose's honor stated the food to be the most superb the kingdom had ever tasted. Tulip kept Snowflake in her lap during the feast, petting him and allowing him to nibble scraps. Rose looked upon this with some sadness. She had shortly discovered after their return that the magic that had accompanied them on their journey was now gone. The sack that provided a bounty of food for their journey now hung empty, the slippers no longer moved with a will of their own, and, heartbreakingly, Snowflake no longer spoke. For all who now met him, he was an ordinary feline and behaved as such. Though, now and again, Rose would believe she caught a glimmer of intelligence in his eyes.

An orchestra assembled, and many danced as others ate. Rose and Joseph entertained her family with some of the adventures they had experienced, though it would be many weeks before they would finish all their tales. With every new story, King Charles and Queen Isabel looked at their daughter with growing respect and pride and looked upon Joseph with endless gratitude. For the most part, Rose's sisters thrilled to her stories, though Daisy looked bored at times. It was during one of the rest periods from dancing that the king announced, to much applause, the formal coronation of Queen Rose of Ametheria would be held the next day. During the proclamation, Rose noticed her mother slip from her seat and walk into a nearby hallway. Silently, Rose followed.

Queen Isabel stood silently in the middle of the hall as Rose approached. She gazed at a large portrait of her mother, Queen Alfreda. This portrait had been oppressive to Rose growing up. Her grandmother seemed to be a large and imposing woman, though, she died before Rose had been old enough to remember her. Now, the portrait reflected something different to Rose, that of a woman of strength who had seen much and had learned great things from it.

Without taking her eyes from the portrait, Queen Isabel spoke. "I was scared."

"Mother?"

Isabel turned to her daughter. "I was not blessed with my Queen Mother's fortitude. Before I learned of my journey, my mother was... demanding. Loving in her way, I suppose, but demanding. As her eldest daughter, she was so disapproving of anything short of perfection from me. There were so many nights I cried myself to sleep because I felt like a disappointment to her. I swore I would not be the mother she was. Then, after my journey, I realized my mother was just doing her best to make me ready for what was ahead in my life.

"When you left, I began to fear I hadn't prepared you as she had me. That in my selfishness to love you and be loved by you, I had endangered you. I am afraid I was not the mother you knew after you left. And when I saw you standing in the courtyard…"

Queen Isabel stopped. Tears fell from her eyes as Rose took her mother's hands in hers.

"Mother, it was your love that prepared me. Not swords, not riding. During my years away, it was your love for me that gave me strength to continue. I would not be here before you now if not for you."

Isabel considered her daughter. "My little girl is gone. Now, I see a queen before me."

"Your little girl will always be here."

The two women hugged. After, Queen Isabel pulled out a kerchief and dabbed her eyes.

"It will be my proudest moment tomorrow seeing you become ruler of our kingdom. I know you will reign with wisdom and compassion."

Rose took her mother by the hand and led her down the hallway. "Speaking of my approaching rule: I may have seen many things and learned much in my time away from my homeland, but I am not wise, Mother. That only comes through time and experience. The crown may rest on my brow, but I would ask you to advise me; to give me the wisdom of your years as a ruler. And, I suppose, father can chime in, now and again."

The two women laughed as they approached a window. They stood there, looking out over the kingdom as it slept under the stars.

"Queen Margaret wished me to send greetings to you," Rose said.

Queen Isabel looked at her daughter puzzled. "Queen Margaret? I am not sure I know..." Her eyes widened and, much like the Queen of Engelbrecht had done when she realized who Rose was, let out a childish, delighted cry. "Princess Margaret! Of Engelbrecht! You met her?"

"Indeed, I did."

Queen Isabel came alive with excited energy. "How is she? Is she well? Has she married? Is she a mother?"

"Yes, to all. She misses you dearly."

Queen Isabel clasped her hands over her heart. "Oh, I miss her, as well. She was such a delight to know. I could not tell you of her because we met on my journey to become queen. Besides, some stories are not very ladylike to tell."

"Oh, I am aware of that, Mother," Rose said as she looked out the window.

Queen Isabel turned toward her daughter. "Rose, did Margaret tell you any stories about me?" she asked.

Rose looked back with a mischievous gleam in her eyes. "Perhaps."

"She did not...she *could not* have told you the one—"

"About the strapping young man bathing in the river?"

Queen Isabel gasped as she put her hands over her mouth, and her cheeks grew bright red. "No!"

Rose smiled. No longer stood her mother in front of her but the high-spirited young lady Queen Margaret had described. "I am afraid so."

Isabel covered her face in embarrassment. "Oh, we were so unkind to that lad, though he did deserve it for teasing the ladies so. It was Margaret's idea, no matter what she told you. That poor man had to climb nearly to the top of that tree to retrieve his garments."

"You received quite the view from what Queen Margaret told me."

Queen Isabel pointed a playful, but stern, finger at Rose as she tried to stifle a laugh. "Not one word to your father, understand?"

"Not one word."

Isabel placed a hand to her forehead as she shook it. "We were so mean. Margaret and I did feel a bit ashamed afterward. I wonder what became of that lad?"

"She married him."

Queen Isabel looked at her daughter wide-eyed before she and Rose burst out in loud gales of laughter.

"There you two are!"

Mother and daughter turned to see King Charles in the hallway. In one hand, he held a goblet of wine, and in the other, much to Rose's surprise, he held Snowflake, who slept. "We all miss you out there. Come join us!"

"Right away, Father," Rose replied. The king, happy as Rose had ever seen him, whispered baby-talk to the cat as he walked back into the ballroom.

"Shall we, Your Highness?" Isabel asked as she held her daughter's arm.

"We shall."

And with that, the two Queens of Ametheria rejoined their family, friends, and subjects as the festivities continued throughout the night and well into the morning.

The End

Special Thanks to all who helped make this book possible:

Tom Boone
Lady Angela Bradley
Xavier & Zoe Campey
Queen Beth Gallagher
Lady Sophia Jung
Sir Jake Larson
Sir Paraag Maddiwar
King Christopher Marksberry
Princess Elizabeth Pompeo
Sir Troy Price
Sam Quinton
Sir Gary Ruschman
Soha Saiyed
Lady Lisa Siebert
And the rest of our KS backers.

Also, a special thanks to Ralph Garman, Eddie Pence and the Garmy for your encouragement.

Jennifer Frazier was born and raised in Northern Kentucky. She obtained a law degree from the University of Louisville and a Masters in Library Science from the University of Kentucky. Jennifer now serves as Kentucky's State Law Librarian and has been featured on the television series "Who Do You Think You Are?".

Daniel Frazier has lived his entire life in the Commonwealth of Kentucky. Daniel began his creative career as a filmmaker and, after directing a feature film, co-created the independent comic book series *The Adventures of Nightclaw & Prowler* which he wrote and illustrated.

Jennifer and Daniel have been happily married for twenty years and are the parents of two children. This is their first novel.

Made in the USA
Monee, IL
08 September 2020